CAROUSEL OF CRIME

Where was Frank? Joe had checked the luggage area and the security office, but there was no sign of his brother. He headed back to the baggage claim area to check once more for Frank.

Joe worked his way through the crowd, searching each face for Frank's. A startled shout made Joe stop and turn. There was some kind of commotion close to the carousel. He pushed his way through the gaping onlookers to the edge of the conveyor belt.

Joe expected to see a suitcase sprung open, spewing somebody's underwear on the floor. He wasn't prepared to see a limp figure in blue coveralls sprawled on the moving carousel. His eyes widened and his heart started to pound as the conveyor belt carried the body closer to him.

Joe instantly recognized the lanky form even though it was facedown on the carousel. It was Frank!

Books in THE HARDY BOYS CASEFILES® Series

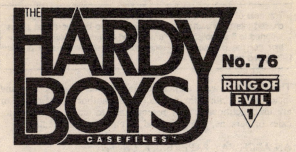

THE **HARDY BOYS** CASEFILES™

No. 76

RING OF EVIL 1

TAGGED FOR TERROR

FRANKLIN W. DIXON

AN ARCHWAY PAPERBACK
Published by POCKET BOOKS
New York   London   Toronto   Sydney   Tokyo   Singapore

This book is a work of fiction. Names, characters, places and
incidents are either the product of the author's imagination or
are used fictitiously. Any resemblance to actual events or lo-
cales or persons, living or dead, is entirely coincidental.

AN ARCHWAY PAPERBACK *Original*

An Archway Paperback published by
POCKET BOOKS, a division of Simon & Schuster Inc.
1230 Avenue of the Americas, New York, NY 10020

Copyright © 1993 by Simon & Schuster Inc.
Produced by Mega-Books of New York, Inc.

ISBN: 0-671-73112-2

First Archway Paperback printing June 1993

10 9 8 7 6 5 4 3 2 1

THE HARDY BOYS, AN ARCHWAY PAPERBACK and
colophon are registered trademarks of Simon & Schuster Inc.

THE HARDY BOYS CASEFILES is a trademark
of Simon & Schuster Inc.

Cover art by Brian Kotzky

Printed in the U.S.A.

IL 6+

Chapter

1

"THIS COULD BE one long summer," Joe Hardy muttered to himself as he stared out the airplane window and half listened to the man questioning his older brother, Frank.

"I don't suppose you two have a lot of experience solving real crimes. Not at your ages," the man said.

Frank Hardy sighed and ran his hand through his dark brown hair. He knew it was no use trying to convince Michael Eddings that he and his brother were experienced detectives. Frank understood how annoyed Eddings must feel at being forced to settle for Fenton Hardy's teenage sons instead of the great detective himself. Eddings's deep brown eyes narrowed as he talked, and a scowl was etched on his face.

Joe glanced at Eddings and tried to control his anger. His father had met the man a few years earlier, when he had done some detective work for Eddings's company, Eddings Air. This time when Eddings needed a private investigator, he flew to Bayport and assumed he could hire Fenton on a moment's notice.

"I wish I'd never gotten suckered into this," Joe mumbled.

Eddings turned to frown at him. "What did you say?"

A warning look from Frank made Joe shake his head. "Just admiring the view," Joe said.

As usual, Frank found himself in the middle, between his headstrong younger brother and the client. Joe, who usually came to life on a case, was grumpy because Eddings didn't have the proper respect for their abilities. He felt the man had ruined his summer vacation plans. As far as Frank knew, though, Joe's only "plans" had been to sleep late every day.

Eddings was unhappy because he hadn't been able to persuade Fenton Hardy to drop the case he was working on and turn his attention to the baggage theft problems that were plaguing Eddings Air. Reluctantly, Eddings had agreed to fly Frank and Joe down to the airline's base of operations, in Atlanta, Georgia—but only to research and check out the baggage operations and security systems. Fenton Hardy would take over the "real" detective work as soon as he wrapped up his current case.

"Remember," Eddings told Frank in a lecturing tone, "at the first hint of danger, you're off the case."

"Crossing the street can be dangerous," Joe blurted out, his blue eyes flashing.

"I just don't want you two blundering into something you can't handle," Eddings retorted.

"We can take care of ourselves," Frank said calmly. "Just because we're still in high school doesn't mean we're impulsive and reckless." As he spoke, he shot a sidelong glance at his brother.

Joe squirmed a little in his seat and smiled behind his hand. Frank had called him both impulsive and reckless on many of the cases they had cracked. He glanced out the window at the city of Atlanta spread out far below. They had been circling for almost an hour because of heavy air traffic at Atlanta's Hartsfield Airport.

Well, if we have to get stuck in traffic, Joe told himself, this is the crate to be stuck in. The flight was pure luxury. They were traveling on Eddings's private jet, which was outfitted with spacious reclining chairs and a sofa,

3

all covered in plush fabric the distinctive blue of the company uniforms and logo.

Although there was room for at least twelve passengers, the only people on the plane were Joe, Frank, Eddings, and the pilot. Eddings, a certified pilot himself, was acting as copilot on the flight. He'd joined the Hardys in the passenger cabin only after the plane went into its holding pattern.

Eddings leaned back against his seat and closed his eyes. Sunlight poured in through the window, bleaching his chestnut skin. "I know we went over everything last night with your father," Eddings said, "but can we go through it one more time?"

Frank leaned forward. Joe nodded vaguely and focused out the window again.

"The thefts started large-scale about six months ago," Eddings began, closing his eyes. "The stolen luggage usually contains valuables like jewelry or cameras. Why we've been hit much harder than other airlines, we don't know. Nobody in the industry has reported losses like ours."

He paused and opened his eyes, looking past Frank to his daydreaming brother. "You can imagine the damage this has done to our reputation," he said loud enough to get Joe's attention. "One of the Atlanta television stations even did a report on our problem a few days ago."

"What kind of security setup do you have?" Frank asked.

"We'll go over the specifics of that later with Hank Forrester, my security chief. He's a top-notch man. He was supposed to come with me to Bayport to brief your father, but he got tied up at the last minute and couldn't make it." Eddings lowered his voice. "Nobody else at Eddings Air knows that we're bringing in an outside investigator."

"We should be getting clearance to land any minute now, Mr. Eddings," a deep voice called from the cockpit.

"About time, Solomon," Eddings yelled back. "I'll be right there."

Eddings got to his feet, straightened his tie, and patted his short-cropped black hair. "The thing I want you boys to remember is that you're here only to do the initial footwork for your father," he said. "Don't get any crazy ideas. I don't want either of you getting hurt. Do you understand?"

"Oh, yes," Frank replied. "We understand perfectly." He saw Joe roll his eyes.

"Boss!" the pilot called out again. "Another ten-minute delay!"

Eddings sighed, rubbed the bridge of his nose, and sat down again. "This is unbelievable. This plane can go four hundred miles an hour, yet all we're doing is flying in circles!"

5

"I've done some flying myself," Frank said. "Could I take a look at the cockpit?"

Eddings sighed again. "Why not? We're not going anywhere for a while."

Frank and Joe followed Eddings to the cockpit. "Solomon," Eddings said as he slipped into the copilot's seat, "I'd like you to meet Frank and Joe Hardy. Their father is a friend of mine, so I'm giving the boys summer jobs to keep them out of their folks' hair."

The pilot glanced back and smiled. "Nice to meet you. I'm Solomon Mapes."

Frank noted that, like Joe, Mapes had blond hair. Unlike Joe, who let his wavy locks do pretty much whatever they wanted, Mapes kept his fair hair slicked down. He seemed to be in good shape, with broad shoulders and muscular arms. His unlined face told Frank that he was still in his twenties or worked very hard at looking young.

"Not too many new employees get to ride in Mr. Eddings's private jet," the pilot said, turning his attention back to the controls.

"I had business in Bayport," Eddings responded a little stiffly, and took his seat. "And, as I said, their father is a friend of mine. Anyway, don't mention this to anybody. Otherwise, everybody will want me to find jobs for their kids."

Mapes raised an eyebrow curiously. "Whatever you say, boss."

Eddings wasn't a very good liar, and Joe could tell that Mapes suspected something was up. The best thing to do, he decided, was change the subject. He nodded at the site below them. "I wouldn't mind paying a visit to the Atlanta Motor Speedway."

"Atlanta's a great town," the pilot said in a distracted tone, his attention on the instrument panel.

"A modern city with a colorful past," Eddings added. "And it looks even better close up. Isn't it about time we got permission to land?"

"We'll just have to be patient and wait our turn," Mapes responded. "Isn't that what you're always telling me?"

"Solomon's not the patient type," Eddings remarked. "He doesn't like waiting." Eddings glanced back over his shoulder at Frank and Joe. He's only been working for me as a pilot for a couple of years, and now he wants to head up the new freight division we're starting."

Frank guessed that Eddings probably admired Mapes's drive. His father told him that Eddings had grown up in a poor family in one of Atlanta's toughest neighborhoods. Now, of course, Eddings headed up his own prosperous airline.

A frown creased Mapes's brow. "The freight division was my idea in the first place."

Eddings chuckled. "And it's a good one,

7

too. But this isn't the time or place to discuss it."

"You boys go back to your seats and buckle up," Eddings told the Hardys. "We should be landing soon."

The boys backed out of the cockpit and took two window seats facing each other in the main cabin.

"At least the delay's giving us a chance to get the lay of the land," Frank noted, pointing out the window at the airport below. "Two main terminals and five concourses that can handle fifty-five million passengers a year."

Joe yawned. "You sound like a brochure— a really *boring* one. Just like this case. Somebody's walking off with a few suitcases. Big deal."

Frank heard a faint whine and felt a rumble under his feet that told him the landing gear was coming down.

"You boys strapped in?" Eddings called out from the cockpit.

"Are we finally going to land?" Joe shouted back.

"Not just yet," Eddings replied. "But when we do, it might be a little rough."

Frank and Joe responded by jumping out of their seats and heading straight for the cockpit.

Frank took in the instrument panel in a single glance. It didn't take him long to figure out what was wrong. "You've got lights on for the rear landing gear but not the front. Is the nose wheel stuck?"

"Either it's not coming down or it isn't locking," Eddings said.

"Trouble either way," Joe responded.

Eddings nodded. He seemed cool enough, and so did Solomon. Frank knew good pilots were trained to keep their cool. He also knew how serious the situation really was. With a lot of luck, a skilled pilot could put a plane down safely without landing gear, but he wasn't eager to test the limits of Mapes's luck or skill.

Mapes pulled the lever for the nose wheel again and again, but the light on the instrument panel didn't blink on. At the same time, Eddings radioed their situation to the tower.

"Only one thing to do," Mapes said after one final pull on the lever. "We'll have to try to release it manually."

"Can we help?" Frank asked.

"As a matter of fact you can." Mapes pointed to the floor behind him. "There's a trapdoor under the carpet that goes below deck to a crawl space." He gestured to the side of the cockpit. "And there's a hand crank in the toolbox over there. It's a fairly simple operation, but it takes a lot of muscle."

"Sounds like my kind of job," Joe responded.

"You're hired," Eddings said.

Frank and Joe rolled back the carpet and lifted the trapdoor. Joe wriggled into the crawl space, clutching the manual crank in one hand and a small flashlight in the other.

Joe rubbed his hands on his shirt and took a tighter grip on the crank. "Here goes!" he shouted back to his brother.

He tugged on the crank. It didn't budge. He squirmed around in the cramped space, trying to get more leverage. He gave the crank another sharp tug and felt a slight movement. Another tug, and ice-cold air rushed in as the hatch started to open. Now the crank was moving easily. Light streamed in through the very small opening and the wheel swung down into place.

"That's it!" he yelled triumphantly when the wheel was all the way down and the crank wouldn't turn any farther.

Joe scooted out of the crawl space, and Frank hauled him back up through the trapdoor. They stood looking at the pilot.

There was a long pause. "Still no light," Mapes said grimly. "You guys better pray that the bulb is just burnt out, because we're so low on fuel we're running on fumes. I'm taking this baby down with or without working landing gear."

Chapter

2

FRANK AND JOE strapped themselves into their seats as the plane began its descent. There was nothing left to do but wait.

Joe stared out the window. He could see fire trucks and ambulances racing along the runway. Joe held his breath, his fingers digging into the plush armrests of his seat.

Joe squeezed his eyes shut and felt a small jolt as the tires hit the pavement. Then a roar filled the plane as the pilot shifted the wing flaps to help slow the jet. Joe opened his eyes. That wasn't so bad, he thought.

"So far, so good," Frank said tersely. He knew the ride wasn't over yet. The plane was still rocketing down the runway at over a hundred miles an hour. If the nose wheel didn't hold . . .

Just then the world tilted at a crazy angle as the plane pitched downward. The agonized screech of grinding metal filled Frank's ears. His body strained against the seat belt. Everything that wasn't bolted down suddenly became a lethal flying object. A coffee mug whizzed past Frank's nose and smashed into the window, shattering into a thousand tiny shards and leaving one long crack in the thick glass.

The right wing hit the ground and sparks flew past the window as the plane started to spin around. Joe felt limp like a rag doll as he was jerked first one way then another. All he could do was grit his teeth and hang on.

He was still grinding his teeth together several seconds after the plane stopped moving. He was waiting for the next surprise. When nothing happened, he decided to start breathing again.

"Next time, I get to pick the ride," he said in a raspy voice. "No more of these roller coasters that feel like plane crashes."

Frank managed to smile. "Are you okay?"

Joe nodded. "And I'm not bored anymore, either."

"Everybody out!" the pilot shouted.

Joe opened his seat belt, jumped up, and

staggered toward the cockpit. "Is anybody hurt in th—"

"I gave an order!" Mapes barked as he stormed out of the cockpit. He grabbed Joe by the shoulders, spun him around, and shoved him toward the hatch.

"Calm down," Eddings said with cool authority. "You did it, Solomon. You got us down safely."

"My job's not done until everybody's off this plane," Mapes countered.

"So let's get out of here," Frank spoke up. He had already opened the hatch and was standing in the doorway.

A fire fighter poked his head inside and scanned the cabin. "Let's go, folks," he said impatiently.

A paramedic herded them away from the crippled jet as fire fighters doused the plane with fire-retardant foam that reminded Joe of whipped cream being shot from a spray can. The crash had almost ripped off the right wing. A trail of motor oil and metal fragments led back down the runway to the jet engine, which had been torn from the underside of the wing.

Joe realized it was a miracle that no one had been hurt. The paramedics apparently shared his opinion and insisted on giving all four of them a quick checkup before whisking them back to the terminal in an ambulance.

"I'd like to take a look at the landing gear," Frank said as the ambulance pulled away from the wreckage.

Mapes glanced at him. "Why?"

Frank shrugged his shoulders. "Call it curiosity. When I almost get killed, I like to know why."

"Don't worry," Mapes responded. "That plane is my responsibility. I'll make sure the company mechanics go over it from nose to tail. We'll find out what went wrong."

Frank decided not to press Mapes. He could tell that Mapes already suspected that he and his brother were more than just summer help, and Frank didn't want to blow their cover before they got started.

A half hour later Frank and Joe were sitting in Hank Forrester's office. Hank, who was Eddings Air's security chief, was a beefy, red-faced man in his fifties, with thinning salt and pepper hair. Forrester stared at the Hardys across his wide desk before shifting his gaze to Michael Eddings, who was standing.

"I couldn't believe it when you called to tell me last night," the man said sourly. "And I still can't believe it now." He waved his hand at the Hardys. "They're just a couple of kids."

"So are a lot of our baggage handlers," Eddings replied. "They'll blend right in."

"That's right, Mr. Forrester," Joe spoke up. "Nobody will suspect that a couple of teenage luggage jockeys are really private investigators."

Hank Forrester's eyes locked on Joe. "Private investigators?" he snapped. "Where's your license?"

"Settle down, Hank," Eddings said evenly. "The boys are just here to do a little advance work for their father." He shot a warning glance at Joe. "Fenton Hardy will do the *real* detective work."

Eddings's assurances didn't satisfy the security chief, Frank knew. He didn't have to be a mind reader to guess that Forrester wouldn't have let them within a hundred miles of this case if not for direct orders from his boss.

Forrester reached into a drawer and tossed a large manila envelope on the desk. "Your ID badges and keys for a rental car are in here," he said flatly. "The car is in the employee parking lot. The license number is on a tag on the key ring. Your bags are already in the trunk."

"We reserved a room for you at the Georgia Inn," Eddings added.

Forrester nodded toward a pile of neatly folded clothes resting on a chair by the door. "Those are your uniforms."

Joe cleared his throat. "Uniforms?"

"If you're going to pretend to be a baggage

handler," Forrester said, "you'll have to dress like one."

Frank smiled and stood up. "Thanks for all your help, Mr. Forrester. We won't take up any more of your time." He headed for the door and stopped to pick up the two pairs of blue coveralls with the Eddings Air logo on the back.

"You'll be working the morning shift, starting at six A.M. tomorrow," the security chief informed them.

Joe was about to groan when Frank cut him off. "That'll be just fine. We'll be there at six sharp."

Joe kept his mouth shut, got up, and followed his brother out of the office.

"Close the door on your way out," Forrester said to Joe.

The Hardys left the small suite of offices that Eddings Air had in the international concourse and wandered out into the main terminal.

"I get the feeling Forrester isn't going to be of much help to us in this investigation," Joe remarked as they strolled along a wide corridor bustling with people either going somewhere or coming back.

"You can't really blame him," Frank replied. "It won't help his reputation if we solve this case." He stopped and glanced around at the fast-food restaurants, magazine stands, and souvenir shops that turned almost every large

16

airport into a shopping mall. "We don't start work until tomorrow morning," he said, handing Joe his uniform, "but we've been on the case since we left Bayport. Let's find out a little more about this airport."

Following signs, they found the escalator that led under the terminal to the subway train that zipped back and forth among the five concourses and the main terminal. The electric train glided quietly to a stop, and the shiny metal doors slid open. The Hardys let the tide of travelers herd them through the doors into the clean, carpeted train.

"Please move away from the doors and toward the center of the car," a robotic-sounding voice said over the intercom.

The doors slid shut, and the train started to roll. "The whole train system is run by computer," Frank told his brother. "No conductors and no engineers."

"No seats, either," Joe observed. As he peered up and down the length of the car, a young woman with short honey blond curls and enormous green eyes caught his attention. She was wearing a blue Eddings Air uniform and seemed to be checking him out.

She smiled and moved closer. "Hi," she said. "How long have you been working for Eddings?"

Joe stared at her, dumbfounded. He and his brother had been in the airport less than an hour, and already a complete stranger knew they were on the case. Joe leaned toward her and whispered, "How did you know?"

She pointed at the coveralls he was carrying. "A dead giveaway," she answered in a hushed tone. "Only guys who work for Eddings Air wear outfits that color blue." Her deep green eyes flashed around the car, and then she leaned closer to Joe. "Why are we whispering?"

Joe smiled with relief. "Oh, I thought you meant—well, never mind what I thought. We just got hired as baggage handlers today."

"We start tomorrow," Frank said, joining the conversation. "I'm Frank Hardy, and this is my brother, Joe."

"I'm Gina Abend," the young woman replied. "I'm a ticket agent. I've only been working for Eddings a few weeks myself."

Her smile widened. "Hey, I've got an idea. Why don't I take you to the employee lounge? You can meet some of your coworkers. I just got off duty."

"Sounds good to me," Joe said eagerly.

Amusement glinted in Frank's eyes. Joe never could resist a pretty girl.

"You go ahead," Frank said. "I'll get our bags and then join you."

Joe stared at his brother. "What do you mean? Our luggage is—"

"Probably collecting cobwebs by now,"

Frank said, cutting him off pointedly. "We should have picked up our bags right after our flight landed, instead of wandering around the airport like a couple of tourists."

Joe got the message. Frank wanted to check out the baggage claim area. "Okay," he said with a slight nod. "But don't take too long. Meet us in the lounge."

Gina explained where it was located.

The automated train reached the last concourse and then headed back. When it reached the baggage claim area, they all got off. Frank waved goodbye to Joe and Gina and followed the signs to the luggage carousels that carried suitcases, boxes, and bags around in circles on conveyor belts. He made a quick stop in a rest room to slip on his blue coveralls before checking out the carousels that handled the bags from Eddings Air flights.

Only a few bags were on the carousel, and no one was standing around waiting. Frank realized that he had shown up during a lull between flights. He stood off to the side and watched several expensive-looking bags go around and around on the carousel. Nobody touched them.

A glint of silver on one of the bags caught his eye. He stepped closer. There was a diamond-shaped silver tag on the suitcase. He glanced around to make sure nobody was watching him, then picked up the suitcase to check the silver tag. It was simply marked Hartsfield/Atlanta, followed by the code AABB45.

As Frank put the suitcase back on the carousel, he noticed that almost all the bags on the conveyor belt had similar silver tags. He stepped back and waited to see what would happen to the unclaimed baggage.

A chubby, red-haired man in Eddings Air coveralls appeared on a motorized cart. He glanced around nervously, then grabbed all the silver-tagged bags and put them in the back of the cart. As he started to drive off, Frank spotted an empty cart nearby. He sprinted over to it and flashed an ID card at the man standing next to the vehicle. "Sorry," Frank said, quickly jumping into the driver's seat. "I've got to borrow this for a minute." He took off before the man could protest.

The other cart turned into a restricted area of the terminal, where only employees were allowed, and Frank followed. He soon lost sight of the redheaded man because he wasn't familiar with the maze of corridors that confronted him.

"I was so close!" Frank said, banging his hands on the steering wheel.

Frank sighed. He decided to return the cart before heading over to meet Joe. Just then he spotted the cart with the red-haired driver coming out of a storage room. The cart was empty now!

Frank waited until the man was out of sight. Then he slipped out of his cart and raced over to the storage room. To his surprise the knob turned easily. He slipped inside.

The room was pitch-black, and Frank groped at the wall for a minute until he found the light switch. He wasn't surprised by what he saw when the bright lights blazed on overhead. The room was full of luggage. He picked up a smooth, black leather bag engraved with somebody's initials. A diamond-shaped silver tag was tied to the handle.

As Frank leaned over to take a closer look at the tag, a scuffing sound behind him made him freeze. Out of the corner of his eye Frank caught a glimpse of a shadow creeping up on him. He spun around to face the intruder and something exploded in his head. A blinding orange starburst blotted out the harsh overhead lights as the world went black.

Chapter

3

JOE WASN'T surprised that at two in the afternoon the Eddings employee lounge was nearly empty. Two young men, both in blue coveralls, were sitting at a table in the corner. They stopped talking and turned to look at Joe when he walked in with Gina.

"Hey, Gina," one of them said. "Got a new boyfriend?"

"Guys, I want you to meet Joe Hardy," Gina responded, ignoring the comment. "He'll be working with you. Joe, this is Danny Minifee."

"Glad to meet you, Joe," Danny said, standing and shaking hands with Joe.

Joe took a quick impression of the stocky,

deeply tanned young man. He guessed Danny was about nineteen, only a couple of years older than Joe. He had sandy-colored curly hair, wide brown eyes, and a broad, friendly face. He spoke with a deep southern drawl, the first Joe had heard in Atlanta.

"I'm Ted Nance," the other guy said. "Welcome aboard. The hours are bad, the pay is low, and the work is tedious. Other than that, this is a great place to work."

Ted was slim, dark-haired, and about the same age as Danny. Joe wouldn't have called him aloof, but there was something in Ted's tone that made Joe feel as if there was some inside joke that only Ted knew about.

"Danny and Ted are both baggage handlers," Gina told Joe. "Maybe they can give you a few tips."

"Sure," Ted responded. "Find another job. That's the best tip I can think of."

"Don't pay any attention to him," Danny drawled. "He doesn't complain on payday."

Ted shrugged. "It's a job. If you work the morning shift like we do, you get off by two. Then you have the whole afternoon and half the night to do whatever you want."

"What about sleep?" Joe responded.

Gina laughed. "Ted usually does that at work."

Ted put his hand on Danny's shoulder. "That's because I have to party for both me

23

and Danny. When Danny isn't hauling suitcases, he's going to college or studying. This
boy is going to be a doctor someday." His
voice took on a heavy, solemn tone. "And
after years of selfless dedication to learning
the healing arts, he'll return to the poor but
honest farming community where he was
raised and tend to the needs of the sick, both
human and livestock, finding a cure for cancer
in his spare time."

Danny's broad face reddened, but he took
the teasing with good nature. "Meanwhile
Ted will stop goofing off," he said, "buckle
down, and take over his father's financial
empire."

"*If* I decide to buckle down and do anything
at all," Ted replied. "For now, my father has
sentenced me to hard labor while I think about
what I want to do."

"The big question in my mind," Joe said,
matching Ted's joking tone, "is whether we
get to keep unclaimed baggage as a fringe
benefit."

Danny's smile faltered.

Ted chuckled as he stood up and stretched
lazily. "I'd keep that idea to myself if I were
you. Management frowns on that sort of
thing."

Danny got up a little stiffly. "We'd better
get back to work or we'll be late."

Ted glanced at the clock on the wall and

sighed. "I don't know why I agreed to work overtime today." He started to follow Danny out of the lounge. "Oh, now I remember," he called back over his shoulder. "We get paid time and a half for overtime."

"They're such opposite types," Joe observed after the two had walked away. "I'm surprised they're friends."

"They're not exactly friends," Gina replied, "but you know how it is when people work together eight hours a day. You either learn to live with each other and get along, or go crazy."

Joe checked the clock. "I wonder what happened to Frank. He should have been here by now."

"It's a big airport," Gina said. "Maybe he got lost."

"You're probably right," Joe responded. "I guess I'd better go look for him." He turned and stared into Gina's big green eyes. "Maybe you should come along to make sure I don't get lost."

Gina smiled but shook her head. "I'm supposed to meet somebody here."

"Too bad," Joe said. "I was hoping we could spend more time together."

"I'm sure we'll run into each other again," Gina said.

Joe grinned. "I'll make sure we do."

*　　*　　*

25

Joe found his way from the employee lounge to the baggage claim area without any problem. There were few people near the luggage carousels, and no sign of Frank, but Joe wasn't worried. Frank knew how to take care of himself.

Where would I go if I were Frank? Joe asked himself. Although the two brothers' minds worked in radically different ways, they somehow managed to reach the same conclusion more often than not. Joe told himself he'd probably start nosing around the security system after he got bored watching suitcases go around in circles.

So he headed back to the security chief's office, hoping that Frank might have gone there to ask Forrester some questions.

The receptionist in the lobby of the Eddings Air office suite gave Joe a dubious glance when he asked to see the head of security. "Didn't I see you in here earlier?" she asked.

"Yes," Joe responded. "But Mr. Forrester asked me to come back here at"—Joe peeked at the woman's watch—"three this afternoon." He leaned over the counter and whispered, "I don't know what this is all about. I hope he doesn't think I had anything to do with those missing hubcaps."

The receptionist pushed her chair back, putting some distance between Joe and herself. "Hubcaps?"

Joe nodded. "All those jumbo jets. Somebody stole all the hubcaps off the landing gear."

"Jumbo jets don't *have* hubcaps," the woman responded, annoyed.

Joe grinned broadly. "Well, then, I guess I'm in the clear. Still, I'd better find out what the big guy wants."

The receptionist picked up the phone. "I'll tell Mr. Forrester that you're here," she said briskly.

A few minutes later Joe was in the security chief's office. Forrester raised his eyes from the computer terminal on his desk long enough to frown at Joe. "What do you want now?"

Joe took one look at Forrester's scowling face and decided this was probably not the best time to reveal that he was having a hard time locating his brother. "I need some background information on standard procedures for tracking lost luggage," Joe said.

"Most bags are located within a couple of days," Forrester told him. "We store all unclaimed bags in a locked storage room next to the baggage claim area. Each item is recorded in a computerized data base that includes the claim check number, any ID tag information, and a physical description of the bag."

"So most people get their luggage back right away most of the time," Joe said.

27

The security chief frowned again. "Most of the time—until about six months ago."

Forrester opened a drawer on the right side of his desk, glanced down, and then tapped a few keys on the computer. He turned the monitor slightly so Joe could see. "When anybody reports a bag as missing, we record that information in the data base, too. If we don't get a match, the entry shows up in yellow. If we still haven't found the bag after a week, the entry changes to red."

Joe noticed that there was a lot of red on the computer screen.

"At first we thought it was a glitch in the system," Forrester continued. "But after we ruled that out, we realized we had a serious problem. This isn't just happening here in Atlanta. Luggage is disappearing from our flights at airports all over the country."

"Do you think any Eddings employees are involved?" Joe responded.

Forrester gave him a weary look. "Since other airlines aren't having similar problems, and since Eddings employees have easy access to the luggage, I'd say it's fairly safe to assume that some of our workers have to be involved in this operation."

Joe ignored Forrester's bitter tone. At least the man was giving him answers. "Do you do any kind of screening when you hire new people?"

"A routine background check is standard procedure, but with the large numbers of people we hire, we don't have the time or the resources to get a detailed profile on each one."

"And all that information is in the computer, too?"

Forrester nodded.

"Just as an example," Joe said offhandedly, "let's say I wanted to find out about a baggage handler I just met, Danny Minifee. What will his file tell me?"

The security chief checked the desk drawer again, where Joe guessed he kept a list of passwords, and then started typing on the computer keyboard. A few seconds later Joe was looking at the personnel file for Danny Ray Minifee.

It was short and simple. Danny was twenty years old. He had been graduated from Porterville High School with a B-plus average and was enrolled part-time at Emory College. He had started working for Eddings Air four months ago. His only previous work experience seemed to be working on the family farm.

Under the heading of "Criminal Record" there was a single word: None. Joe knew that cracking this case was going to be a lot harder than checking the personnel file of the first guy he met. Still, it had been worth a shot.

29

Forrester twisted the computer monitor away from Joe's eyes. "You shouldn't see confidential files," he said gruffly. "I don't know what got into me, I must be putting in too many hours." He nodded toward the door. "The sooner you get out of here, the sooner I can get back to work. If I'm lucky, maybe I'll get out of here before midnight for once."

Joe couldn't think of any other questions to ask Forrester, and he wanted to find Frank. He murmured his thanks and headed back to the baggage claim area to check for his brother again.

This time there was a large crowd standing around one of the carousels. Glancing at a video display terminal on the wall that listed departures and arrivals, Joe noticed that an Eddings Air flight had just landed. The passengers jockeyed for positions close to the carousel to wait for their luggage to appear.

Joe worked his way through the crowd, searching each face for Frank's. A startled shout made Joe turn. There was some kind of commotion close to the carousel. He pushed his way through the gaping onlookers to the edge of the conveyor belt.

Joe had expected to see that a suitcase had sprung open, spewing somebody's underwear on the floor. He wasn't prepared to see a limp figure in blue coveralls sprawled on the moving carousel. His eyes widened, and his heart started to pound as the conveyor belt carried the body closer to him. Joe instantly recognized the lanky form even though it was facedown. It was Frank!

Chapter

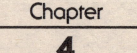

4

"FRANK!" JOE SHOUTED. He leapt onto the
moving carousel and crouched down next to
his brother. "Turn this thing off!" he yelled.

Joe was only vaguely aware of the people
staring at him as the conveyor belt continued
around in its endless circle. His attention was
focused on his brother. The only movement
from Frank was the slight rise and fall of his
back. At least he was alive and breathing, Joe
told himself. He was out cold, though, and
Joe knew not to move him. It might be
dangerous.

Joe glanced up at the strangers crowding
around the luggage carousel. "Somebody turn

this thing off!" he shouted urgently. "Find an emergency switch! Do something!"

Somebody finally got the message, and the carousel ground to a halt. "Get a doctor!" Joe heard a woman call out.

"Joe!" another voice cried out. "What happened?"

Joe spotted Danny Minifee crawling through the opening where the conveyor belt fed out of the loading area.

"Who is this guy? What's wrong with him?" Danny asked, puzzled.

"He's my brother, Frank," Joe told him.

At the mention of his name, Frank's eyes fluttered open, and he stared up at his brother. "Joe?" He tried to get up.

"Just lie still," Joe said, putting a hand on Frank's shoulder. "A doctor or paramedic should be here soon."

Frank shook off his brother's gentle grip and struggled to sit up. "I don't need a doctor," he insisted. A sharp pain shot up his head from the base of his neck. He let out a soft groan and rubbed his sore neck with one hand. "What happened? How did I get here?"

Joe looked up at Danny. Two other guys in blue coveralls had joined him. "That's a good question," Joe said, staring at Danny. "Maybe one of these guys saw something."

All three of them shook their heads.

Danny knelt down next to Frank and Joe.

"We were just bringing in a load of bags when we heard somebody hollering about an emergency and stopping the carousel. I hit the shut-off switch and came running."

"This is Danny Minifee," Joe told his brother. "I met him in the employee lounge earlier."

"These other guys are Abel Cantu and Evander Renshaw," Danny said.

Frank smiled weakly. "Sorry we had to meet under such strange circumstances."

"Hey, Danny," one of the two men said. Frank wasn't sure which name went with which face. "We'd better get back to work. People are waiting for their luggage."

"Are you going to be okay?" Danny asked Frank.

"My head hurts," Frank responded, "but other than that, I'm fine. Just give me a hand off this thing and you can start it up again."

Joe and Danny helped Frank climb off the luggage carousel, and then Danny went back to the loading area. When the carousel started moving again and suitcases began to roll out, the small crowd lost interest in Frank and turned back to the important task of pouncing on their bags.

A paramedic team showed up with a stretcher and an emergency aid kit. Frank faded into the stream of travelers, pulling his brother with him.

"You really should let those guys take a look at you," Joe protested as they moved away from the baggage claim area.

"There's no time for that," Frank insisted. "We have to get back on the trail before it gets cold." He told Joe about his discovery in the storage room. "We've got to get security down to that storage room right away. Whoever whacked me on the head isn't going to wait around to see if I tell anybody about the stash of stolen luggage. They'll move the stuff out as fast as they can."

The Hardys headed straight for the Eddings Air offices, brushed past the startled receptionist, and burst into the security chief's office.

"What is it now?" Forrester barked as he rose out of his chair.

Frank quickly repeated his story. Forrester listened in silence, tapping a pencil on his desk the whole time.

"So you saw some luggage in a storeroom," Forrester said, "and got conked on the head. From that you conclude that you uncovered a secret cache of stolen bags and were attacked by one of the culprits.

"But you don't know if the bags were stolen," the security chief continued, "and you didn't actually see anybody hit you. Are you sure you didn't just bump into something?"

"Oh, right," Joe retorted hotly. "Then he staggered out of the storage room, made it all

35

the way to the baggage carousel, and keeled over onto it." He turned to his brother. "Let's go. We'll bring back some of the evidence and stack it up in here."

"Now, hold on," Forrester responded, his voice rising. "At this point I'm ready to follow any lead—no matter how slim. Show me this pile of loot you found."

Frank led the way. He made a few wrong turns in the maze of corridors but finally found the storeroom. He knew it was the right one because the motorized cart he had commandeered earlier was still parked nearby. "This is it," he said, gesturing to the closed door.

Joe tried the door. "It's locked."

"That's strange," Frank said. "It was open when I was here before."

Forrester pulled a large key ring out of his suit-coat pocket, flipped through the assortment of keys, slipped one into the lock, and pushed open the door. Murky darkness greeted them.

Frank brushed past the security chief and hit the light switch on the left-hand wall. The harsh overhead lights glinted off the sparkling clean linoleum floor, revealing a wide-open space with absolutely nothing in it.

"This is exactly what I was afraid would happen," Frank said bitterly. "We wasted too much time. They've already moved the stuff."

Forrester shook his head and sighed. "I

know you boys are trying to help, and maybe you *can* help if you stick to the program." He directed his gaze at Frank. "I wouldn't mention this little incident to Mr. Eddings if I were you."

"Why not?" Frank responded.

"Because if you tell him your wild theory about stumbling on a storeroom filled with stolen luggage, I'll have to tell him what I think *really* happened."

Joe glared at the security chief. "And what's that?"

Forrester kept his eyes on Frank. "You were nosing around the luggage carousel, accidentally whacked your head on something, and imagined the rest."

"Is that a polite way of calling me a liar?" Frank asked in a cool voice.

"I don't think you're lying," Forrester replied. "I just think you're a little overeager and that blow to your head scrambled your memory. Sometimes our minds play tricks on us."

"Not mine," Frank said evenly.

Forrester sighed and glanced at his watch. "Now if you'll excuse me, I have work to do."

Forrester ushered the Hardys out of the storeroom, locked the door, and strode off down the corridor.

"I'd like to get back in there and check out

the space for clues," Joe said after the security chief was out of sight.

"I doubt if we'll find anything," Frank replied. "That room wasn't just emptied out; it was cleaned out. The floor was still wet in a few places where it had been mopped."

Something on the ground caught Joe's eye. He bent down and picked it up. "Hey, Frank, remember those diamond-shaped luggage tags you told me about?" He handed Frank a silver tag. "Is this one of them?"

"What are you guys doing back here?" a voice called out.

Frank and Joe peered down the corridor and saw Solomon Mapes, the pilot who had flown Michael Eddings's private jet. Joe immediately noticed that Mapes wasn't alone. He had an arm around Gina Abend.

"What are *you* two doing here?" Joe responded lightly, trying to hide his disappointment at the way Gina was clinging to the pilot.

"We were looking for you," Mapes answered. "You guys certainly get around. First, I find out that you've already met my girlfriend. Then I hear you were playing tag on one of the luggage carousels. Finally I run into Hank Forrester, and he tells me some wild story about an invisible stash of stolen luggage."

Joe felt a rising anger that Forrester had revealed so much.

"I thought I saw a guy stealing luggage,"

Frank said, "and I thought he hid the bags in this storeroom. So I figured I'd score some points by reporting it to the chief of security. Instead, I wind up looking like a complete idiot. The room was empty."

Not bad, Joe thought. Frank had managed to tell enough of the truth to make the story believable and not blow their cover.

"We've heard that there's been a big problem with luggage thefts around here the last few months," Joe contributed. "We figured we could track down the bad guys in our spare time and get a bonus."

Gina smiled. "Sounds like fun. I always wanted to be a detective."

Joe looked away from her big green eyes. "Well, we probably won't have time for that now. Our new jobs should keep us pretty busy."

Frank nodded. "We start training first thing in the morning." He held out the silver luggage tag. "Does this look familiar to either of you?"

Gina shook her head.

Mapes scrutinized the tag. "Never saw one like it before. Anyway, the reason I came to find you is to tell you the news."

"What news?" Joe asked.

"A preliminary check of the landing gear on Mr. Eddings's plane came up with a possible reason for the landing gear failure. It's pretty weird. In fact, I'm sure a more thorough check will come up with a more logical explanation.''

"Why don't you give us the weird version," Frank responded.

"I'm getting to that," the pilot said. "It seems that somebody might have tampered with the landing gear."

Joe's eyes narrowed. "Do you mean sabotage?"

Mapes shrugged. "I know it sounds crazy, but there were two bolts missing from the front landing gear. There was no way the gear could lock for a safe landing."

Chapter

5

"SABOTAGE?" Gina exclaimed. "All of you could have been killed!"

"It doesn't make any sense," Mapes said, shaking his head. "Who would want to kill Mr. Eddings?"

"Maybe he wasn't the target," Joe ventured.

Mapes stared at him. "What do you mean? Do you think somebody is after you?"

Frank quickly covered for Joe's near-blunder. "No, of course not," he said quickly. "What about you? Do you have any enemies?"

The pilot laughed. "Me? I may rub some people the wrong way, but I don't think anybody hates me enough to bump me off. No, I think the attempt, if it was one, must have been on Mr. Eddings."

41

"Have you told him yet?" Frank asked.

Mapes shook his head. "No. I don't want to ring any alarms until I'm absolutely sure."

"So why are you telling us?" Frank responded.

Mapes shrugged. "I guess I wanted to tell *somebody*. And since you guys were on the plane, I figured you had a right to know."

Joe heard a low beeping coming from either Gina or Mapes. "Either one of you has a watch with an alarm, or you've got a concealed microwave and your popcorn is ready."

Mapes pulled a small metal object out of his pocket. "It's my beeper. I'd better call in." He walked back up the corridor, and Gina went with him.

"Let us know if you find out anything else," Joe called after them.

Gina swiveled her head to peer over her shoulder. "And you let me know before you chase any more bad guys. I want to get in on the action."

The next morning Frank was up before the sun. By five-fifteen he was dressed and ready to go. By five-thirty he had hounded Joe out of bed and into his clothes, even though Joe was basically asleep on his feet. They got to the airport a few minutes before six and reported for work right on time.

They spent most of the morning in a training

class with several other new employees. The only part that interested Joe was when they got to drive the baggage tugs that hauled the luggage to and from the big jets. With three or four baggage carts hooked behind the tug, Joe felt as if he were driving a miniature, trackless train.

At ten A.M. they got a "lunch" break and wandered into the employee lounge. Joe was just peeling the plastic wrap off a mystery sandwich when Danny Minifee and Ted Nance walked into the lounge.

"Hey, guys," Danny said, greeting them with his friendly smile. "How do you like the job so far?"

Joe shrugged. "We haven't actually done any work yet, so I can't complain."

"Frank, you met Danny Minifee yesterday," Joe said. "And this is Ted Nance, another baggage handler."

"Nice to meet you," Frank said, shaking Ted's hand.

"I see you've decided to try our exotic cuisine," Ted said, nodding at Joe's sandwich. "I think they load the vending machines with food the inmates at the county jail refuse to eat."

Joe eyed the grayish substance between the two wafer-thin slices of bone-white bread. He was hungry—but not that hungry.

Ted chuckled as Joe tossed the sandwich

43

into the nearest trash can. "Sorry. I didn't mean to spoil your appetite."

Danny turned to Frank. "How are you feeling? Is your head okay?"

Frank rubbed the sore spot on the back of his neck. "Let's just say I'm in much better shape now than when we met yesterday. Thanks again for your help."

"I was just doing my job," Danny said.

Ted groaned. "Captain Modesty strikes again! Cantu told me about how you practically flew off the tug and hit the carousel's emergency shut-off switch. The other guys were still standing around wondering what all the shouting was about while you were racing down the conveyor belt. If you're going to be such a fired-up go-getter, at least learn to make it pay off for you."

"You would have done the same thing," Danny contended.

"Probably," Ted conceded. "But I would have tried to weasel a reward or a bonus out of it. You're not exactly rolling in dough, my friend, and your college tuition isn't cheap."

"Tell me about it," Danny muttered. "If I don't find a roommate to split my rent with me, I'm going to have to move out of my apartment."

"How about two roommates?" Frank asked. "We need a place to stay."

Joe stared at his brother. The hotel where

they were staying was very comfortable, and it had a nice, big swimming pool. He started to object but held back because he knew what Frank was doing. This was a great opportunity to get close to Danny. Maybe he could provide some clues for the case.

Danny's face brightened. "Great! Meet me here when the shift's over, and I'll show you the apartment. It needs a little work, but there's plenty of room for three."

"That's because you don't have any furniture," Ted remarked.

When the break was over, Danny and Ted went back to loading luggage, and Frank and Joe went to a lecture on the many hazards and safety regulations involved in hauling baggage around an airport.

"I didn't know lugging suitcases around could be so dangerous," Joe whispered to his brother. "I'll try to remember not to stick my head in any jet engines."

The training class ended a few minutes after two, and the Hardys found Danny and Ted waiting for them at the employee lounge.

"The apartment only has two bedrooms," Danny said as they strolled out to the parking lot. "So you guys will have to share. I hope that's okay."

"No problem," Frank said.

"What about beds?" Joe asked, thinking about the comfortable mattresses at the hotel.

"I'm sure we can find something at a second-hand store," Danny replied. "Until then, a couple of sleeping bags on the floor is about the best I can offer."

"Sounds okay to me," Frank said cheerfully. "We don't mind roughing it for a few days. Right, Joe?"

Joe forced a smile. "Uh, right. You bet."

They came to a sleek, red Corvette. Ted fished a set of keys out of his pocket, unlocked the driver's side door, and slipped inside.

Joe let out a low whistle. "Nice set of wheels."

Ted shrugged. "The gas mileage is lousy." He turned the key in the ignition, the engine roared, and Ted drove off, waving goodbye as the convertible top rolled back and folded itself down behind the bucket seats.

"The car was a high school graduation present from his father," Danny explained. "Ted flunked out of college after the first semester, and his old man's so mad now, he won't give him a penny. That's why Ted's working here. If I had a car like that, I'd sell it and use the money to help pay my tuition."

"School's really that important to you?" Frank asked.

"I'm the first in my family to go to college," Danny responded. "Everybody back home is sort of counting on me. My high school grades were good but not good enough for a scholarship. That's why I'm working, too."

He gave the Hardys directions to his apartment and climbed into a rusty pickup truck. The engine needed quite a bit of coaxing before coughing and rumbling fitfully to life.

Frank and Joe watched Danny drive away in the old truck. "He seems like a really honest and open guy, doesn't he?" Frank mused.

Joe nodded. "Either that, or he's very slick."

The Hardys went back to the hotel in their rental car, showered, rested a bit, and packed their luggage. Then they followed Danny's directions past the new housing developments that had grown up around the airport to an older area of Atlanta with tree-lined streets. As they neared their destination, Frank noted that the well-worn charm of the sprawling old homes gradually gave way to neglect.

"Big house," Joe commented as they parked in front of the address on Magnolia Avenue that Danny had given them.

"But who knows how long it'll remain standing," Frank said, taking in the sagging porch roof and the faded and peeling paint. "From the way Danny described his place, I don't think he rents this whole house. It must be split up into apartments."

47

Joe checked out the other houses. Most of them were in pretty bad shape. "This is definitely a low-rent neighborhood. If Danny is involved in the theft ring, he's not getting rich from it."

Danny's apartment turned out to be in the back of the house, on the first floor. He took them on a quick tour of the four small rooms. Joe suspected that the ancient stove and refrigerator in the kitchen would be worth more as decorative antiques than as working appliances. Moving into the living room, Danny dropped onto a worn-out couch and invited Frank and Joe to sit on a couple of chairs that could have been rescued from a trash dump.

"Well, at least we won't have to worry about burglars," Joe remarked. "There's nothing in here worth stealing."

"I'm kind of on a tight budget," Danny said a little sheepishly. "Maybe the three of us can pitch in together and fix the place up a little."

Someone banged on the front door. "Let us in!" a voice shouted.

Danny opened the door, and Gina, Solomon Mapes, and Ted Nance crowded into the apartment. Joe's attention was drawn to the stack of pizza boxes in Ted's hands. The spicy scent wafting from the boxes reminded Joe that he had hardly eaten anything all day. He was starving.

"Ted told us you were moving in with

Danny,'' Gina said. ''So we decided to have a little welcoming party.''

Ted plopped the boxes on the floor and tore open the top one. Within seconds half the pizza was gone and they all stood around chomping on thick slices that oozed hot cheese.

Frank noticed that Solomon Mapes seemed a little uncomfortable. He didn't really fit in.

After a couple slices of pizza, Frank got thirsty and wandered into the kitchen to see if there was anything to drink. He found a six-pack of soda in the refrigerator and took out a can. When he turned around, he found Mapes standing in the kitchen doorway.

''I'm afraid I was a little out of line when I mentioned sabotage yesterday,'' Mapes said.

Frank frowned. ''You think the damage to the landing gear was accidental?''

''We found a broken-off piece of one bolt in the nose wheel housing. The other bolt could have worked loose, causing too much stress for the remaining bolt to handle.''

''Well, I guess that makes more sense than sabotage,'' Frank replied. Or was it the work of a professional who knew there'd be an inspection after the accident? he wondered. He didn't mention that idea to Mapes because the man seemed determined to play down the possibility of foul play.

''Anyway,'' Mapes said, ''I just wanted you

and your brother to know it was probably just an accident." Then he walked back into the living room, leaving Frank alone in the kitchen.

Frank remembered the unopened can of soda in his hand and pulled the pop top. Soda foamed out of the opening and dripped onto the floor. The foam kept bubbling out of the can as Frank rushed over to the counter. He tossed the can in the sink, but not before half the soda inside had found its way onto the floor.

Searching for a towel or something to mop up the wet, sticky mess, Frank rummaged through the kitchen cabinet drawers. The first drawer was full of cheap silverware. The second one held a jumbled assortment of utensils. The third drawer yielded a checkered dish towel.

Frank pulled out the dish towel, froze, and stared down in stunned surprise. The towel had concealed a sealed plastic bag in the bottom of the drawer—and the bag was bulging with silver, diamond-shaped luggage tags.

Chapter

6

FRANK STARED at the silver tags. They were clean, with no airport codes written on them. What were they doing here? Did this mean that Danny was somehow involved in the luggage theft ring?

Frank needed to talk things over with Joe. He quietly closed the drawer and mopped up the spilled soda. Then he went back to join the others in the living room.

Joe was curious, wondering why it had taken Frank so long to get a soda.

"We need to get our stuff out of the car," Frank said to his brother.

"Need any help?" Danny asked.

"No thanks. We don't have that much,"

51

Joe responded, knowing that Frank must want to talk to him in private.

Outside, a soft dusk was beginning to fall, enveloping Atlanta's beautiful old trees and aging homes in the hazy glow of a southern sunset. Frank was glad they had decided to stay at Danny's apartment instead of a hotel. He wasn't sure where the silver tags would lead them, but they sure wouldn't have turned up in a hotel room.

"What's up?" Joe asked as they walked toward the car. "Did Mapes tell you something?"

"No," Frank replied. "It wasn't anything Mapes said. It was what I found in one of Danny's kitchen drawers—a whole pile of those silver luggage tags."

"You're kidding!" Joe hated the idea of Danny's being involved in the theft ring.

Frank shook his head. "I wish I was. I like Danny. We'll just have to see where this lead takes us. There's always a chance that somebody planted those tags to frame him."

Carrying their bags, they made their way slowly back inside, both considering the next step they should take.

Early the next morning when Frank and Joe reported for work, they met Bob Briggs, the burly crew chief.

"I get some students on summer vacation

in here who don't know what it means to take a job seriously." Briggs eyed them challengingly. "We work hard here and expect you to do the same."

"Yes, sir," Joe replied. He resisted the impulse to make a joke, sensing that Briggs wouldn't appreciate it.

"Good," said Briggs. He turned to Frank. "And no more riding on the luggage carousel. This isn't an amusement park."

"Yes, sir," Frank answered quickly.

"Okay," Briggs said. "Minifee! Get over here and show Rookie Number One how it's done. Nance, you take the other one."

Frank figured he must be Rookie Number One. That was okay with him. By being split up, both he and Joe could cover more ground.

During the course of the morning, Frank grumbled about the hard work and joked about the rocks that the travelers must be packing in their bags to make them so heavy. Danny laughed. When Frank went on to suggest that there must be a quicker, easier way to make money, Danny pointedly ignored the remark.

On the other side of the baggage area, Joe was making similar remarks while he stacked luggage onto a tug to transport to another flight.

"Someday I'll find a way of getting rich

without having to work so hard," he complained to Ted.

"Do you think I'd be working as a baggage handler if I could get my hands on easy money?" Ted said with a laugh. "If you find some, let me know."

It was a long morning, but Frank and Joe were in good shape, and the work, though boring, wasn't difficult. At Joe's insistence, they avoided getting their lunch from the vending machines, opting instead to eat at a snack counter in the airport. They ate quickly, using the rest of their break time to familiarize themselves with the airport and its routines.

In the afternoon, when their shift ended, they compared notes as they walked to their car.

"Security's pretty tight," Frank pointed out. "Slipping luggage out shouldn't be that easy."

"It might not be that hard for someone who's worked here long enough to be trusted," Joe replied. "Maybe as long as you're wearing an Eddings uniform, you can blend in so nobody'd notice you."

As they made their way across the parking lot, Frank saw someone standing next to their rental car. Frank grabbed Joe's arm and nodded in the man's direction.

"What's Forrester doing there?" Joe asked as they approached the security chief.

They stopped a few feet from the car.

"Raise the hood," Forrester directed. "Let's check out the engine."

Frank paused, then unlocked the car and released the hood.

"What's going on?" Joe questioned Forrester.

"That's what I want you to tell me. We're going to pretend that you're having car trouble and I'm helping you out. Gives us a chance to talk without your being seen hanging around my office," Forrester explained. "I'd like a progress report."

"We haven't been—" Joe started to complain.

"Basically we've spent our time making connections," Frank interrupted. "We've moved in with a coworker named Danny Minifee, and we've gotten together with a few other Eddings employees." He purposely avoided reporting the stash of silver tags he had discovered. He wanted to check things out a little more before implicating Danny. "We're keeping our eyes open and spreading the word that we're not exactly happy with base pay. We'll see what happens."

"That's it?" Forrester snorted.

Frank ignored the comment and continued, "It would be a big help if we could get access to the computerized personnel files. It would save us a lot of time."

55

"Sorry." Forrester straightened up. "Can't be done."

"Why not?" Joe asked. "You showed them to me before."

"That was a mistake. Those records are confidential. Besides, I've already gone through them. There's nothing in there that could help you." Forrester slammed down the hood and stepped back. "Glad to see you boys are doing so well," he said with obvious sarcasm. "Maybe when your dad gets here, we'll get some real detective work done. That is, if I haven't solved the problem by then." He stomped back to the airport terminal.

"He likes us a whole lot," Joe grumbled.

Frank grinned. "Maybe he just doesn't like detectives who haven't finished high school yet."

"Maybe he isn't very good at what he does and is afraid we'll show him up," Joe said.

The expressway was fairly crowded with fast cars, but Joe enjoyed driving even if their little rental car was short on horsepower.

"He did this on purpose," Joe groaned as he coaxed their reluctant car out into traffic.

"What are you grumbling about?" Frank asked.

"Forrester," Joe responded, "purposely rented the slowest car in the lot for us. I have this lemon floored, and we're not at the speed limit yet."

"Oh, gee, Joe," Frank chided, "you mean it'll take us a whole five minutes longer to get to Danny's apartment?"

Joe glanced in the rearview mirror and frowned. "Someone's following us."

"Which car?" Frank said, craning his neck to peek over his shoulder at the traffic behind them.

"The dark red Lincoln, two cars back. Watch," Joe said as he moved over to the left lane. The Lincoln did the same.

"I wonder who it could be?" Frank remarked.

"Let's try to find out." Joe abruptly exited the highway. From the rearview mirror he could see the Lincoln skidding to make the lane change and causing quite a few angry beeps from other cars. Frank held on to the armrest as Joe turned sharply at the bottom of the exit ramp. The Lincoln came much too fast down the ramp, not even bothering to slow for the yield sign.

"At least you can't complain about the steering," Frank remarked as Joe swung the car down another street.

"Yeah, who needs video games when you can have a good car chase down crowded city streets?" Joe replied. The car behind them made the corner and picked up speed. Frank turned around to study it. Its large size gave the impression of its being a shark about to gobble up a smaller fish. Deep tinting on all the windows and mud conveniently splattered all over the license plate made identifying their pursuer impossible.

"Can you get a look at them?" Joe asked.

"No way. That tinted windshield turns them into two big blobs," Frank replied.

"How big?"

"Big enough. Step on it!"

Joe skidded around the next turn, onto a one-way street. He was bent over the wheel, concentrating hard on the road. The monstrous Lincoln almost overtook them, pulling up along the passenger side of the vehicle. Frank pressed his face close to the glass in an attempt to identify the driver. He could tell that it was a large man with short hair, but the man's features were distorted by the dark glass.

"He's crowding us toward the curb!" Joe shouted.

"Joe, look out! We're going to hit that parked car!" Frank yelled over the screeching of tires. At just the right moment, Joe managed to make the little car leap ahead, squeezing between the parked car and the Lincoln.

Frank checked again. The Lincoln had accelerated and was almost beside them. The driver-side window lowered a crack to show a glint of metal.

"Get us out of here!" Frank shouted frantically. "He has a gun!"

Chapter

7

JOE TOOK HIS EYES off the street for a second to glance over at the pistol barrel protruding out the window of the big sedan. He was close enough to see that it had a homemade silencer.

The pistol spat blue fire. A muted *thwip* was followed a split second later by a loud *boom*. The Hardys' rented car bucked and swerved, thumping over the curb and smashing past a trash can.

"He shot out one of the tires!" Joe shouted, wrestling with the steering wheel. A towering steel lamp post loomed in front of the car. Joe cranked the stiff, unresponsive wheel with all his strength and slammed on the brakes. The car veered back onto the street, spun around, and skidded to a halt.

Frank twisted his head around and caught a last glimpse of the sedan as it screamed around a corner and disappeared.

Joe popped the trunk release, jumped out, and grabbed the lug wrench out of the trunk. It wasn't much of a weapon, but he wasn't going down without a fight if the Lincoln came back. His heart was hammering in his chest, and every muscle in his body was taut, ready to explode into action.

"I think we're in the clear now," Frank said after a long, tense minute had passed.

Joe kept both hands tightly wrapped around the lug wrench. "I don't get it. We're sitting ducks. Why didn't they come back and finish us off?"

"I don't think that was part of the plan," Frank replied. "At point-blank range, the shooter didn't hit the tire by accident. That's what he was aiming at. I think this little encounter was meant to scare us off the case."

Joe seemed to notice the heavy iron tool in his clenched fists. "Well, since I've already got the lug wrench," he said, relaxing his grip, "we might as well change the tire."

Frank rolled out the spare tire. "You know, I really hate getting shot at—especially when I don't know who's doing the shooting."

"I don't think the bullet holes are any smaller when you know who made them," Joe responded as he slid the jack under the car.

"Still, I know what you mean. The only suspect we have now is Danny Minifee, and that definitely wasn't Danny's pickup truck.

"And even if Danny is involved with the theft ring," he added, "I just can't see him going along with a stunt like this."

Frank took the lug wrench and loosened the lug bolts on the ruined tire. "There's something else we have to consider."

"What?" Joe asked.

"Unless this was a random, drive-by shooting, somebody in the operation knows we're on the case."

"But only Eddings and Forrester know that," Joe said.

"They're the only ones who know that we're *officially* working on the case," Frank corrected. "Gina and Mapes know that we dragged Forrester down to that empty storage room."

"That's right," Joe said. "And let's not forget whoever it was who whacked you on the head and dumped you on the luggage carousel."

Frank nodded. "So now we have a nice long list of suspects. All we need is a few clues to narrow the field and some solid evidence to wrap up this case."

They finished putting on the spare, threw the dead tire and tools in the trunk, and drove to Danny's apartment, where they found Ted Nance and Danny in the living room.

"It took you guys long enough to get home from work," Ted observed. "Were you out seeing the sights, or did you make a wrong turn somewhere and get lost?"

"Somebody didn't like the way I was driving," Joe replied. "So he ran us off the road and shot out one of our tires."

"Shot!" Danny stared at them in open-mouthed surprise. "Are you sure?"

"Well," Joe said, "the guy waved a gun at us, and then the tire went blooey. So, if he didn't shoot out the tire, it was an amazing coincidence."

Frank studied Ted for a moment. Joe's news didn't seem to faze him at all. "Does this kind of thing happen a lot around here?" Frank asked him.

Ted shrugged. "You know how it is. Atlanta has its share of big-city problems. Maybe you were just in the wrong place at the wrong time." He paused and grinned. "Or maybe you snore too loudly and Danny decided to get rid of you."

"You should know," Frank responded in a joking tone. "The two of you were together when it happened."

Ted shook his head. "Don't look at me. I just got here." He looked over at Danny. "If you need an alibi, I'd cheerfully change my story for fifty bucks.''

"Very funny," Danny said, clearly not amused. "Hey, I almost forgot. There was a phone call for you guys a little while ago."

"Who was it?" Frank asked.

"He wouldn't tell me. He gave me a phone number and said you should call as soon as you got in." Danny handed Frank a sheet of paper with a phone number scribbled on it.

Frank went over to the phone and dialed the number.

"Michael Eddings," a brisk voice announced on the other end of the line.

"Uh—yes," Frank said, glancing over at Ted and Danny and shrugging as if he had no idea whom he was talking to. "This is Frank Hardy. I got your message."

"I want to see you and your brother as soon as possible," Eddings told him.

"Okay," Frank replied.

"I have to go to a meeting right now," Eddings said, "and you probably shouldn't come to my office, anyway. Somebody might see you. I should be home by about eight. There's a park across the street from my house. Meet me there at eight-thirty."

Eddings gave Frank his address and general directions to his house. "We'll be there," Frank assured Eddings as he filed the informa-

63

tion in his brain. He didn't want to write down anything that Danny or Ted might see.

"It's really nice of you to invite us, Mrs. Miller," Frank added after Eddings hung up. Frank put down the receiver and groaned loudly. "You're not going to believe this, Joe. That was one of Aunt Gertrude's friends. She lives in Atlanta, and she wants us to come visit her—tonight."

Joe caught the glint in Frank's eye and suspected that the caller had never met their aunt. "Do we have to?" he moaned, playing along.

"You know Aunt Gertrude," Frank said. "If we don't go, we'll never hear the end of it."

Frank glanced at his watch as Joe pulled the car over to the curb next to a lush green, shady park. It was almost eight-thirty. The summer sun hung low in the western sky, casting long shadows on the road from the big houses across from the park.

The Hardys got out of the car and walked into the park. Frank spotted a tall, thin man sitting on a bench next to a duck pond. "There he is," he murmured to his brother. They joined Eddings on the bench and waited for a few evening joggers to pass.

"Some detectives you are," Eddings said in a low, sharp voice when they were alone.

"You've only been here a couple of days, and already you've lost your cover."

Joe was startled. "What are you talking about?"

"Forrester tells me that missing luggage is suddenly showing up on baggage carousels at airports all over the country," Eddings said. "It's clear that the ringleaders of the operation are onto you and have decided to lie low while you're on the scene."

"It also means we're getting close," Joe countered. His eyes shifted to his brother. "Tell him about the luggage tags."

Frank told Eddings about the diamond-shaped silver luggage tags he had seen on the bags in the storage room and in Danny Minifee's kitchen. "I don't know if Danny is part of the luggage theft ring," Frank concluded, "but some of the baggage handlers must be involved. They have more access to the bags than anybody else."

"And that's not all," Joe interjected. "Your life could be in danger. That 'accident' with your plane may have been sabotage."

Eddings stared at him. "What do you mean?"

"Didn't Mapes tell you?" Joe responded. "He thinks that somebody may have tampered with the landing gear."

"Hold on a minute, Joe," Frank said. "Mapes changed his story. He told me that the bolt might have fallen off accidentally."

"Come on," Joe objected. "Do you really believe that?"

Frank shook his head.

"Listen, Mr. Eddings," Joe said. "If the sabotage theory is true, then the people running this operation aren't about to let anything—including you—stand in their way."

Eddings stood and stared silently at the pond for a minute. "I'll have to look into this," he finally said. "In the meantime, why don't you see what you can find out from Minifee—but be careful. I'll talk to you again soon."

Frank and Joe waited until Eddings was out of the park before they got up off the bench and headed back to the car. They drove around for a while to kill some time. When they got back to the apartment, Joe entertained Danny with a story about their fun-filled evening with the imaginary Mrs. Miller, who Joe claimed was a retired army drill sergeant who bombarded them with recruiting brochures.

About an hour later Solomon Mapes showed up at the door. He spoke to Danny in a low tone, and then Danny announced that he was going for a walk.

"I wanted to have a word with you two in private," Mapes explained after Danny left.

"So now we're alone," Frank responded. "What's up?"

"I got a call from Mr. Eddings tonight," Mapes said flatly. "He wanted to know why I hadn't told him that his plane might have been sabotaged."

"And why hadn't you?" Joe asked.

"Because I told Frank that I thought it might have been an accident," Mapes replied.

"And now?" Frank prodded. "Are you ready to come to a conclusion?"

"I had one of our top mechanics examine that broken bolt," Mapes said. "He thought somebody might have sawed partway through it."

"Just far enough so the plane could take off and land a few times before the bolt snapped," Frank ventured.

Mapes nodded. "But I can't prove it." He glanced down at his watch. "I have to get going. I just wanted to give you guys a little advice. Stick to your jobs and don't ask a lot of questions about things that are none of your business. You could get hurt."

Joe's eyes narrowed. "Is that advice or a threat?"

A troubled look passed over Mapes's face. "Call it whatever you want."

Joe crawled into his sleeping bag a few minutes after midnight and was fast asleep in less than a minute. It seemed that he had just shut his eyes when a heavy pounding startled him awake. The faint predawn glow in the window told him it was almost time to get up to go to work.

He pulled the sleeping bag over his head and closed his eyes again. He wasn't going to move until Frank, the human alarm clock, bullied him into getting up.

The insistent pounding assaulted his ears again.

"Who is it?" Joe recognized Danny's sleepy voice from the other bedroom. "What do you want?"

Joe sat up and saw that Frank was out of his sleeping bag. "Come on," Frank whispered. "Let's find out what's going on."

Joe started to complain as the noisy *thud, thud, thud* was suddenly joined by the crack of splintering wood. "Somebody's trying to break down the door!" he exclaimed.

Joe jumped to his feet, too, and raced after his brother to the front door, where they were joined by a startled-looking Danny. A final heavy blow smashed into the door, ripping a chunk of the door frame out of the wall. The door flew open, and a half dozen shadowy figures burst inside.

Chapter

8

JOE WAS TENSED for action but didn't make a move. Four men and two women, all armed, faced them. This was not the time for hasty action, considering the intruders were dressed in the uniforms of the Atlanta police.

"What's the problem?" Frank asked.

Before anyone could speak, Hank Forrester strode into the room, acting even more self-important than usual.

"Good job, boys," Forrester said to the police officers.

Joe wondered how Atlanta's finest men and women felt about being called boys.

"We have a warrant to search this apartment," Forrester said. "You'll have to let us look the place over."

"We'll take care of this, Mr. Forrester," one of the female officers said. Forrester, obviously annoyed, stepped back. "Who's Daniel Minifee?" she asked.

"That's me," Danny replied, stepping forward.

"What are the grounds for this warrant?" Frank asked the closest officer as the warrant was handed over to Danny.

"I can tell you," Forrester boasted. "Eddings told me about that bit of evidence you found here. So I did a little checking and found out that Minifee had been arrested for armed robbery once. It happened when he was a minor, and the charges were dismissed, which was why the information didn't show up in the routine check before he was hired."

"What are you looking for?" Danny asked.

"Silver tags that we have reason to believe are being used in the luggage—ah, here they are now," Forrester said as a police officer walked up to them carrying the bag full of silver tags.

"Those aren't mine," Danny protested. He was fully awake now, red-faced and angry. A second police officer displayed a valuable-looking gold watch, a diamond bracelet, and a small ruby ring.

"I suppose these aren't yours, either," Forrester looked at Danny.

"N-No—I've never seen them before," Danny sputtered.

"I believe these items are among those reported missing. Would you like to explain how they got here?" Forrester questioned.

Danny didn't respond. While Frank and Joe stood by watching helplessly, Danny was read his rights, handcuffed, and led away.

"I didn't do anything," he yelled back to Frank and Joe.

They were alone with Forrester now.

"What I don't understand," Frank said, "is why you went to all this trouble. If Danny is working for the ring, he's probably just a minor player. I thought our goal was to shut down the entire operation and catch the leaders."

Forrester's chest puffed out. "This is where experience counts, my boy. I know when to make a move and what the results most likely will be."

"What do you mean?" Joe asked.

"Minifee should be so scared he'll start talking and give the whole thing away. Even if he doesn't, the ringleaders will think that he has. That should rattle them enough to shut down their operation. We'd like to catch them, but the most important thing is to stop the thefts."

71

"I can't believe this," Joe muttered as Forrester turned and left the apartment.

Frank agreed. "I really doubt that a highly profitable, well-organized ring of thieves would shut down because of one small arrest."

Joe nodded, leading the way into the kitchen. "I'm hungry," he announced. He opened the refrigerator door. A couple of slices of dried-out pizza stared back at him. "But not that hungry."

Frank didn't seem to hear. He sat down at the kitchen table. "The way I've got it figured is that ticket agents or baggage handlers at airports across the country spot expensive-looking luggage. They put the silver tags on those bags, rerouting them to Hartsfield. Naturally, the luggage is unclaimed so a member of the ring can pick up the bags. They put the luggage in storage until they can get it out of the airport unnoticed."

"Sounds like a reasonable theory," Joe agreed, "except Eddings told us that bags have stopped disappearing since we arrived. And we haven't been here that long. With bags being sent from all over the country, how could they stop the action that fast?"

"Easy," Frank explained. "All they have to do is remove the silver tags when the bags arrive here. What you have left is just a bunch of misrouted luggage, which would be taken to the unclaimed luggage area, entered into the computer, and eventually returned to its owners.''

Frank stood up and nodded toward the clock on the wall. "So much for a full night's sleep. We have to report to work soon.''

On the way to work the Hardys stopped at an all-night diner for some breakfast. They shared their disappointment that Danny was involved in the thefts.

"I couldn't help liking the guy," Joe said as he dumped pepper all over his eggs and greasy hash browns. "And all my instincts told me he was innocent."

"He says he is, and I'd like to believe him, too," Frank agreed. "But instincts don't count in court. Evidence does. And so far, all the evidence was at his place."

Joe nodded. "We should both be on the lookout for those silver tags—while they're still attached to the luggage."

They arrived at the airport a few minutes early. Bob Briggs saw them and motioned them over. "You two mind going on the clock a little early? We're shorthanded and the work is already piling up."

"Shorthanded?" Frank asked casually.

"Looks that way. Danny and Ted were both scheduled to start an hour ago, and neither one has shown up or bothered to call."

73

Briggs shrugged. "And we have a particularly heavy day today. Anyway, with both of them out, you two will work together. Go ahead and clock in—and thanks."

"I didn't agree to start early," Joe grumbled, his eye on the doughnut shop across the airport terminal.

Frank rolled his eyes and changed the subject. "We know where Danny is, but don't you think it's strange that Ted is out today, too?"

"Maybe he just overslept," Joe responded as he stifled a yawn. "I can understand that."

"Maybe . . ." Frank nodded, lost in thought. "Look over there," he whispered as they approached the baggage area.

Joe looked in the direction Frank indicated. Among a pile of suitcases was a particularly extravagant piece of luggage. It was a long, slim, and elegantly hand-tooled leather case. Joe guessed it to be one of a kind. He gave out a long, low whistle. "Someone has a nice fishing-rod case here," he commented.

"*Had,*" Frank pointed out as he tentatively lifted a rather smelly green duffel bag that was weighting down the back end of the fishing-rod case. "Obviously it's been stolen." He indicated the silver tag attached to the leather handle.

"Pay dirt!" Joe exclaimed, and began rummaging through the rest of the pile to see if there were any more. Within a few hours they had discovered seven more bags with the distinctive silver tag.

"No one's taken off the tags," Frank observed.

"That could be because the guy who's been removing the tags is in jail," Joe replied. "And don't forget, Ted's missing, too. He could also be involved."

"I've been thinking about that," Frank agreed as he moved two bags marked for Houston to the appropriate conveyor belt.

"So, what do we do next?" Joe asked.

"I have a plan."

"Don't say that." Joe eyed his brother warily. "Your plans always have me doing something stupid."

"Let's take the marked bags to that storage area where I first saw the stash of luggage," Frank continued, oblivious to Joe's protests.

"Why? So we can both get bashed on the head this time?" Joe responded.

Frank smiled and checked his watch. "It's time for our break. Let's go." He began pulling out the silver-tagged bags and placing them on a carousel. Joe reluctantly joined him, admiring the fishing-rod case as he placed it with the others on the belt. They quickly left the loading area, told Briggs they were taking their break, then entered the baggage claim area where passengers were picking up their luggage. Frank spotted an unattended motorized cart and hopped into the driver's seat. Joe jumped on the back as Frank got it going. They drove to the carousel they had just loaded, discreetly but quickly grabbed the silver-tagged bags and tossed them onto the cart. They then drove their stolen cargo to the empty storage room. No one stopped them. No one seemed to notice them.

They had just put the last piece of luggage in the room and were about to race back to work when Frank heard footsteps behind him. "What do you two think you're doing?" a threatening voice demanded.

Chapter

9

JOE DROPPED the bag he was holding and whirled around. His mind was racing, searching for a plausible excuse for why he and his brother were hiding a pile of expensive luggage in an unused storage room.

"Gina!" Joe gasped the name with relief when he realized she was the one who had caught them in the act. "I'm glad it's only you."

"*Only* me?" she said with a slight pout.

Joe grinned. "You know what I mean."

Gina frowned as she took in the storage room. "I'm not sure I do. What are you guys doing?"

"That's a little hard to explain," Frank responded.

"I think maybe I can figure it out for myself," Gina said. She made a face at Joe. "You're playing detective again, and you left me out."

"We've got a plan to trap the guys who've been stealing luggage," Joe admitted.

"We can't say any more than that right now," Frank cut in.

"Okay," Gina said, obviously disappointed. "But if there's anything I can do to help, just let me know."

"As a matter of fact, there is," Frank replied as an idea came to him. "Can you get access to the computerized personnel files?"

Gina's gaze turned away from him and wandered around the room. "Gee, Frank, I don't think so," she said. "My computer access is limited to the reservations system. I doubt if I could get anywhere near the personnel records."

"Too bad," Frank said. Gina seemed upset by his request, so he decided not to press the issue.

"Well," Gina said, "I guess I'd better get back to work."

Joe watched her walk down the corridor. "Too bad she's taken," he muttered, shaking his head.

"Come on, Joe," Frank called. "We're

going to have to find another place to stash this stuff."

Joe stared at him. "Why?"

Frank picked up the leather fishing-rod case and tossed it in the cart. "Don't you think it's a little strange that Gina was wandering around the storage area? I don't see too many passengers checking in down here. Do you?"

"Gina?" Joe reacted in a startled tone. "Come on, Frank. You're starting to think everybody's a suspect."

"Everybody *is* a suspect," Frank said flatly. "You forget that sometimes." He picked up another bag and piled it in the back of the cart. "Let's get moving."

Frank spotted a room full of cleaning supplies and decided that would be a good place to store the luggage. He and Joe hid the stash in a corner behind a couple of waist-high barrels of industrial detergent. Then Joe grabbed some more supplies and stacked them on top of the bags. Unless someone was looking for the bags, they wouldn't be noticed.

"There's only one thing about this plan that bothers me," Joe remarked as they headed back to work.

"What's that?" Frank responded.

Joe looked over at his brother. "What do we do now?"

"Now we go on a fishing trip," Frank answered. "We dangle the bait to see what kind of fish bites."

"I see," Joe said, even though he didn't. "And what kind of fishing line do we have tied to this bait?"

Frank smiled. "One of the oldest lines in the book. 'We've got something you want. How badly do you want it?' "

Joe returned the smile with a grin of his own. "I get it. We drop a few hints here and there. Then we sit back and wait for the bad guys to come to us."

There was one problem with the plan, Frank realized at the end of the work shift. "We hardly know the other baggage handlers," he said to Joe as they walked out to the parking lot. "We spent all our time with Danny and Ted. Now Danny's in jail, and Ted's not around.

Joe nodded. "I made a couple of passing remarks to Cantu and Renshaw, but I wouldn't exactly call them friends."

Frank was silent for a moment, lost in thought. "Just because Danny's locked up," he finally said, "doesn't mean he can't talk to anybody. He can have visitors, right?"

"That's right," Joe agreed. "And if we have a little talk with him, he could pass that information along to somebody else."

"What are we waiting for?" Frank said. "Let's head over to the jail."

A short while later Frank parked their car in front of the county jail. It was a cold, imposing hunk of gray concrete. A uniformed police officer at the front desk took their names and told them to wait, nodding toward some uninviting orange molded plastic chairs. A few minutes later he called the Hardys back up to the desk.

"You're too late," the officer told them. "Your friend's already out on bail."

"Are you sure?" Joe asked. "I didn't think Danny had enough money to make bail."

"One of his friends put up the money," the officer responded.

Frank raised his eyebrows. "Who?"

"Sorry, we don't give out that information," the officer responded. "But I can tell you the guy probably had money to burn. He kept asking me how long it was going to take because his Corvette was double-parked outside and he didn't want to get a ticket."

Joe waited until they were back outside to say, "Something tells me that Danny knows only one person with a Corvette—Ted Nance."

"The way Nance talked, though," Frank responded, "you'd think he was just as hard up for cash as Danny."

"I'm surprised Ted would go to the trouble to bail Danny out," Joe said.

"Unless they're both in this together," Frank ventured. "Ted might be afraid that Danny would talk."

They drove back to Danny's apartment and discovered that all his personal stuff was gone. His closet was empty, and his textbooks had been cleared out of his bedroom. Frank noted that even the cheap manual typewriter that Danny used for his homework had vanished.

"Either we're dealing with a very selective and not very bright burglar," Joe said, "or our friend has moved out."

"My guess is he went back home," Frank said. "What was the name of that town?"

"Porterville," Joe answered, remembering the name of the high school Danny had graduated from on Forrester's computer.

Frank rummaged around in his travel bag and pulled out a Georgia road map. "Here it is," he said, pointing to a tiny speck. "It's about ninety miles south of Atlanta." He glanced at his watch. "We'll go down there in the morning."

"Ted's family lives right here in Atlanta," Joe responded. "I remember how surprised I was that he lives with them even though he tries hard to reject them. Why don't we visit him tonight?"

In the phone book, Frank found the Nances' home address. A half hour later the Hardys were getting out of their rental car in front of a three-story, modern brick-and-glass house with a wide, manicured lawn and a fenced-in tennis court.

"Nice place," Joe remarked as they walked up to the front door. "At least we know that Danny told the truth when he said Ted's family had money."

He pushed the doorbell, and deep, rich chimes rang inside the large house. A uniformed maid answered the door and let them in after Frank explained that they were Ted's friends. She left them standing on the marble floor of the foyer while she went to announce them.

Joe tilted his head back and stared at the high, vaulted ceiling. "I'd hate to have to pay to heat this place."

"This is Atlanta," Frank reminded him. "It never gets very cold here."

"Oh, right," Joe mumbled.

A tall woman with white hair, dressed in a tailored gray business suit, came into the entrance hall. "I'm Helena Nance," she introduced herself. "I'm Ted's mother."

Frank took her outstretched hand. "I'm Frank Hardy, and this is my brother, Joe. We work with Ted at Eddings Air."

"I see," she said in a reserved tone.

83

"Ted didn't show up for work today, and he didn't call in," Joe said. "We wanted to make sure he was all right."

"He's not sick, if that's what you mean," Mrs. Nance responded. "But I don't know if he's all right. When I got home from my office, I found him throwing some clothes into a suitcase. He seemed very upset about something. When I asked him what was wrong, he told me he was old enough to take care of himself. Then he stormed out of the house. I have no idea where he went!"

Having failed to locate Ted, Frank thought it was even more important now to find Danny and talk to him. So Frank was up and ready to go at four the next morning.

Joe was definitely *not* ready to go, but Frank dragged him along, anyway. "It's too early," Joe complained as Frank drove south toward Danny's hometown in the predawn haze. "Everybody will still be in bed."

"It'll be two hours later by the time we get to Porterville," Frank countered, "and people get up early in the country."

"Two hours!" Joe groaned. "I don't suppose we could stop and get something to eat on the way?"

Frank chuckled. "It's too early. Nothing's open. But we'll probably find some kind of restaurant or coffee shop in Porterville. We'll stop there, have breakfast, and see if we can get directions to the Minifee farm. If we're lucky, we may find some folks who can tell us something about Danny."

"Good plan," Joe said, "especially the part about breakfast." Then he drifted off to sleep.

Joe didn't wake up until Frank turned off the highway onto a side road. Five minutes later they were in Porterville. Less than a minute after that they had gone from one end of town to the other. Joe counted one stoplight, four stores, two gas stations, and one restaurant.

Frank pulled into the parking lot of the Porterville Café. When the Hardys walked through the front door, every head in the restaurant turned to look at them. There was a moment of dead quiet, then the customers went back to eating and talking.

Frank and Joe sat at the counter and ordered breakfast. When the waitress brought their food, Frank casually mentioned that they were looking for Danny Minifee.

"I don't believe I've heard that name before," she said with a thin smile. "You must have the wrong town. Maybe he lives in *Pot*terville. That's about seventy miles from here. People get the two confused all the time."

Joe watched as the waitress moved down the counter to another customer. "I don't think we're going to get much help here," he said to Frank. "These folks aren't going to open up to a couple of outsiders."

By the time they finished eating, the restaurant was nearly empty. Frank was about to ask for the check when a short, round man approached them.

"I heard you say you were looking for Danny Minifee," he said, glancing around the restaurant. "What kind of trouble is he in now?"

"What makes you think he's in trouble?" Frank responded.

"I'm Roger Starke," the pudgy man said. "I run the grocery store down the street." His eyes darted around the room again, and he lowered his voice. "That boy is crazy, if you ask me, and dangerous, too."

Joe couldn't believe what he was hearing. This man couldn't be talking about the same Danny Minifee, not the Danny that Joe knew. Maybe Joe didn't know Danny at all. Now was the time to find out about the *real* Danny Minifee.

Chapter

10

FRANK STUDIED the jumpy little man. "What makes you think Danny Minifee is dangerous?"

"He tried to kill me once," the man claimed as he sat down on the stool next to Frank. "Back when his old man got sick and I gave his mother a job. I couldn't pay her as much as my regular workers. I only hired her because I wanted to help the family out, and I'm not made out of money!" the man shouted, pounding his fists on the counter.

"Hey, take it easy, mister," Joe cautioned.

"One day the kid shows up at the store waving a shotgun around," the man continued in a lower voice. "He accused me of cheating his mother out of what she had rightfully earned. Imagine that!"

Joe had no problem imagining what he'd do if he found out some tightwad store owner had taken advantage of his family's hardship to hire cheap labor. "So what happened?" he asked.

"The judge bought Minifee's story and gave him a suspended sentence." Starke shook his head slowly. "The way I see it, the law's too soft.

"Anyway," he concluded, "I just thought you should know." His eyes flitted around nervously again. Then he got up and abruptly left the restaurant.

"I don't believe a word of that guy's story!" Joe declared.

"That's good," another voice replied, "because there wasn't much truth in it."

Joe turned to see the waitress standing a few feet away. "What do you know about it?" he asked.

The waitress sighed. "Everybody in town knows about the bad blood between Danny Minifee and Roger Starke. Danny was only about fifteen at the time. The two of them had words, and Danny *was* carrying his father's shotgun—but it was still in the case. I think he was taking it to the hardware store for some repair work."

The three of them talked for a few more minutes, and the waitress finally agreed to give the Hardys directions to Danny's house, which was only a short drive out of town.

Frank couldn't help thinking the farm was a little like Danny himself, neat and unassuming. The white frame house had been painted recently, and rows of bright flowers lined the side of the house and walkway leading to the front door. Frank wasn't surprised to see Danny's pickup truck parked down near the barn.

They found Danny fixing an old tractor. "I figured somebody would come looking for me," he told them. "But I didn't think it would be you. What are you doing here?"

"We want to help you," Joe replied.

"Tell us everything you know about the luggage theft operation," Frank said.

Danny's expression hardened. "I never stole a single piece of luggage."

"But you know people who did," Frank prodded.

Danny fixed his eyes on the ground. "I wasn't sure until yesterday. When Ted bailed me out, he admitted that he was responsible for that stuff that the police found in the apartment."

Joe stared at him. "He *told* you that he planted the jewelry and the silver tags?"

Danny nodded. "And he was the one who knocked you out, Frank."

Joe frowned. "Why would Ted go to all the trouble to frame you and then bail you out?"

Danny shrugged. "Ted's not really bad. He just got in too deep with some bad people. It was all a game to him until I got arrested. When he realized I might get convicted and sent to prison, he tried to undo the damage."

"You mean he went to the police and confessed?" Frank responded.

"Ted?" Danny laughed. "No, he's probably halfway to Mexico by now. He promised to write a letter clearing me. That's about the best I can hope for." Danny smiled. "You must think I'm a real dumb country boy."

"No," Frank said. "I think you're a pretty smart guy, and the smart thing to do is go back to Atlanta and tell the police what you know."

"What do you think this is?" Bob Briggs bellowed when Frank and Joe showed up very late for their shift. "Some kind of vacation resort?"

"Sorry," Joe said. "We ran into a little traffic." He left out the minor detail about the small detour that took them almost two hundred miles out of the way.

"It won't happen again," Frank assured the foreman.

Briggs scowled. "If we weren't already shorthanded, I'd fire you on the spot. I added some guys from the other shifts, but you two had better pull more than your weight if you want to keep your jobs. And I expect you to work overtime to make up some of the time you missed this morning," he added.

Joe forced himself to smile. "No problem, boss."

After four hours of nonstop lifting and loading, Joe decided that it was, in fact, a fairly major problem. At the end of their regular shift, he wanted to find a place to lie down and go to sleep for about a day. He had to settle for a ten-minute break.

Joe trudged into the employee lounge with his brother. He had just gotten a soda from one of the vending machines when Gina walked in.

"I just heard about what happened to Danny," she said as she sat down at the table with Frank and Joe. "Arrested for stealing luggage! I can't believe it."

"Neither can we," Joe replied.

Frank shot a warning look at his brother. "Have you seen Ted Nance lately?" he asked Gina. "He didn't show up for work yesterday or today, and he didn't call in sick."

"I hope he's okay," Gina said.

"I hope he's still in the country," Joe muttered. Frank kicked his brother's shin under the table.

Gina's eyes widened. "Do you think that Ted was involved in the luggage theft ring with Danny?"

91

"What do *you* think?" Frank responded.

Gina shrugged. "I never thought about it until now. Everybody knew Danny was desperate for money for college. But all Ted has to do is sit back and wait for his father to cool off, and then he'll have enough money to do whatever he wants. Why would he steal luggage?"

"Good question," Frank said. He turned to his brother. "Time to get back to work."

Joe was a little perturbed at Frank's tight-lipped routine every time they saw Gina, but he didn't get a chance to bring up the subject. Bob Briggs hollered for them to hurry up and join a crew that was loading bags into a waiting jumbo jet.

The work was simple, and Frank and Joe had both gotten the hang of the routine. Standing on either side of the mobile conveyor belt that angled up from the ground to the belly of the big bird, they quickly got into the rhythm of pulling suitcases off the luggage carts and throwing them on the conveyor belt. Another baggage handler grabbed the bags at the top and stacked them in the plane's cargo hold.

Frank noticed the catering truck that had just pulled up behind his brother. He was fascinated by the elevator platform that the truck used to lift the heavy steel food carts up to the plane.

"We're running out of time," Joe said, and

Frank pulled his eyes away from the catering truck. "If the guys running the luggage theft ring haven't already shut down the operation completely, they'll probably move it to another airport or switch their ID system."

"I know," Frank said. "But I don't know what we should do next."

Frank glanced up at the catering truck. An attendant was pushing the food carts from the elevated platform into the plane. Suddenly the catering truck lurched backward, just inches behind Joe.

Frank's attention was riveted on the attendant and the fully loaded food cart. The man was trying to grapple back from the gaping chasm that had opened between the edge of the elevated platform and the loading hatch of the plane.

The heavy cart teetered on the edge. Frank knew the attendant couldn't hold it. The cart ripped free of his struggling grasp and hurtled down—right toward Joe's head!

Chapter

11

"LOOK OUT!" Frank shouted as he stretched across the luggage conveyor belt to grab hold of Joe's blue coveralls. Frank clutched the fabric as he yanked his brother off the ground and onto the moving conveyor belt.

The runaway food cart from the elevated platform smashed into the ground right where Joe had been standing. Plastic trays flew through the air. Frank was only dimly aware that something soft splattered on his chest. Someone shouted nearby. Frank barely noticed.

"Joe!" he called out as the conveyor belt carried his brother up toward the belly of the plane. "Are you okay?"

Joe stared down at Frank in stunned confusion, wondering why his brother had mixed vegetables and mashed potatoes smeared all over the front of his uniform. He heard people yelling and spotted the food cart lying on its side on the asphalt and swallowed hard as he took in what had happened. Frank's split-second reaction had saved his life.

Somebody finally stopped the conveyor belt before it dumped Joe in the cargo hold, and he scrambled back down to the ground. He joined his brother and a group of other workers around the crumpled metal cart.

The man who had been loading the carts into the plane lowered the elevator platform and rushed over. "Are you all right?" he asked Joe. "I'm really sorry. I tried to hold the cart, but it all happened so fast."

Joe glared at the man. "Do you expect me to believe this was an accident?"

The man gave him a startled look. "What are you talking about? Of course it was an accident. Why would I do something like that on purpose?"

"That's what I'd like to know," Joe retorted, his hands curling into fists.

Frank put his hand on his brother's shoulder. "Hold on, Joe. I saw what happened. Don't blame this guy. Somebody moved the truck while he was putting the cart on the plane."

The three of them walked around the catering truck to the driver's side. The door was wide open. The cab was empty.

"What's going on here?" a voice bellowed behind them. Frank turned to see Bob Briggs rushing across the pavement.

Frank and Joe told Briggs what had happened. The burly foreman nodded his head gravely. "You boys go home and get some rest. You must be pretty shaken up." He paused and scratched his head. "I've never seen an accident quite like this before."

"It wasn't an accident," Joe insisted forcefully. "Somebody deliberately moved the catering truck while it was being unloaded."

"You don't know that for sure," Briggs said calmly. "But I'll see to it that Hank Forrester is informed. We'll let him handle it."

Briggs turned to Frank. "Take your brother home. He's had a rough day."

Frank took hold of Joe's arm and got him moving. "The man just gave us the rest of the day off," he said. "Don't argue."

"Why is Briggs suddenly being so bighearted?" Joe muttered as he and his brother moved out of earshot of the crew boss.

"He sure seemed determined to get us away from the scene in a hurry," Frank replied. "If I wanted to cover up a phony accident, the first thing I'd do is make sure there weren't any witnesses hanging around."

"Do you think Briggs moved the catering truck?" Joe asked.

"Even if he didn't, he might be involved. Remember, this luggage theft ring is a big operation. And this isn't the first time someone tried to scare us off. Don't forget about that little drive-by shooting."

Joe nodded. "So what do we do now?"

Frank thought for minute. "Let's do exactly what he told us to do. Go back to the apartment and get some rest. We've been up since four. A couple hours of sleep wouldn't hurt."

"I'm too tired to argue," Joe said.

Frank was opening the apartment door as the phone rang. Joe darted in and grabbed the receiver while Frank was still taking the key out of the lock.

"Hello?" Joe said.

"Hardy?" A gruff voice spoke in the phone.

"Who wants to know?" Joe responded cautiously. He didn't recognize the man's voice.

"I don't have time to play twenty questions," the voice snapped. "We want those bags you took."

"What's going on?" Frank whispered.

Joe held up his hand. "What are you talking about?" he asked the man.

"You know what I'm talking about. Now let me tell you something you *don't* know."

97

The man's voice was cold and menacing. "That little accident today was just a sample of what happens to people who cross us."

"What is it?" Frank whispered urgently.

Joe covered the receiver with his hand. "Somebody finally took the bait. They want the luggage we snatched."

"Stall," Frank advised.

Joe spoke into the phone. "We'll see what we can do. What's it worth to you?"

"Your lives," the icy voice replied.

"Oh," Joe said. "That sounds like a deal we can live with—but it'll take us some time to get the luggage."

"Tonight," the man stated flatly. "We'll contact you."

A sharp click on the line ended the conversation abruptly.

Joe hung up the phone slowly and turned to his brother. "That guy knew we took the bags. And there's only one person who saw us doing it." The name stuck in his throat.

Frank nodded. "Gina."

The Hardys left the apartment and headed back to the airport. When they got there, they went to the check-in counters assigned to Eddings Air in the main terminal.

"I don't see her anywhere," Joe said.

Frank walked up to one of the ticket agents on duty. "Hi, Stacy," he said, reading her name tag and acting as if they were old friends. "We're looking for Gina. Have you seen her?"

The woman looked at him uncertainly. "You mean Gina Abend?"

Frank nodded. "Of course. Who else would I mean?"

"I—I don't know," the woman said hesitantly. "Do I know you?"

Frank ignored the question. "She must have forgotten she was supposed to meet us and went home already." He started to leave, but then stopped and turned back to the ticket agent. "Hey, Stacy. I don't have Gina's home phone number with me. Could you get it from the computer?"

The woman laughed. "Nice try. If you want Gina's phone number, you'll have to get it from her."

Frank smiled and shrugged. "You can't blame me for trying."

"I know where we can find Gina's phone number and address," Joe said as they walked away from the check-in counters.

"I do, too," Frank responded. "Forrester's personnel files."

Joe glanced at his brother. "Do you think he'll let us see Gina's file?"

"I doubt it," Frank said. "But he might be willing to tell us where she lives. Let's give it a try."

The stiff receptionist at the Eddings Air offices gave them a frosty reception. "Mr. Forrester is out of the office at the moment. Can I take a message?"

Joe glanced around in a secretive way and leaned across the counter. "It's all right. Nobody can hear us. We can drop the cover."

"Wh-what are you talking about?" the woman stammered.

"Swordfish," Joe whispered.

The woman stared at him blankly.

"You know," Joe prodded. "The password. Swordfish."

The woman blinked.

"He didn't tell you?" Joe reacted with dismay. "He assured us that we could count on you! Oh well, we'll just have to take a chance and trust you." He turned to his brother and whispered, "Forrester has a list of passwords in his top right desk drawer." He continued out loud for the receptionist's benefit, "You go check the chief's office. I'll sweep this area."

The woman reached for the phone as Frank walked briskly toward the security chief's office.

"Good idea," Joe declared, snatching the receiver from her grasp. "The first place to look for bugs is the phone system. We'll make a first-class operative out of you yet."

Frank slipped into Forrester's office and closed the door behind him. He turned on the computer and found the list of passwords right where Joe said it was. After a few false starts, he found the password that opened the personnel records, and soon had Gina's file on the screen.

What he saw created more questions than it answered. Gina's address was there, and so was the date she was hired. Other than that, the file was completely blank. No references, no previous employers, no school records. Nothing.

Frank scowled at the screen. He made a quick scan of a few other personnel files. Gina's was the only one without any of the typical background information that Frank had expected to find. What made Gina a special case?

"Don't go in there!" Frank heard his brother shout. "There's no telling what might happen if you disrupt the hypersonic electrodebuggerizer!"

Frank quickly shut off the computer, realizing that Joe's act was just about played out. He opened the door to find the startled receptionist reaching for the knob.

"All clear," he announced as he brushed past her.

"Good!" Joe exclaimed as they hurried away from the office, leaving the bewildered woman hovering on the threshold of Forrester's office, peering cautiously inside.

Frank told Joe about what he'd found as

they left the airport and drove to the apartment complex that was listed as Gina's address.

"Joe! Frank!" Gina exclaimed when she opened the apartment door in response to Joe's insistent knocking. "How did you know where I live?"

"You don't sound very happy to see us," Joe observed. "In fact, you sound a lot like you did the other day when we asked you to help us get access to the personnel files."

Gina looked down at the floor. "You know, don't you?"

"We know that there's something strange about your file," Frank said.

"How did you find out?" Gina asked. "Forrester didn't let you see my file, did he? No, he wouldn't do that."

"Why wouldn't he?" Joe prodded.

Gina sighed. "You've gotten this far. I might as well tell you the whole story. I paid Forrester to give me a clean slate. Before I got this job, I had some lean times and had a hard time paying the bills. I wrote a few bad checks and got caught once for shoplifting. That's all, nothing major."

"But enough to prevent you from getting a job at Eddings Air," Frank noted.

Gina nodded. "I'm not some kind of criminal. I bribed Forrester so I could get a job.

I'm not involved with anybody stealing anything. I swear."

"You were the only person who knew that we took a load of stolen luggage and hid it," Frank said. "Now somebody else knows. Who did you tell?"

"I didn't tell anyone," Gina said defensively. She paused for a second. "Except for Solomon."

Frank and Joe looked at each other. Frank remembered the "advice" Mapes had given them in Danny's apartment: "Stick to your jobs and don't ask a lot of questions about things that are none of your business. You could get hurt." Now the reason for the veiled threat was becoming clear.

Chapter

12

"WHY DID YOU tell Mapes that we took the luggage?" Frank asked Gina.

"I'm sorry," Gina replied. "I guess I just wasn't thinking. Solomon and I are close. We don't keep secrets from each other. I didn't think I was doing anything wrong."

Joe walked over to the window and stared out at the city. "I used to have someone special in my life," he said softly. "I know how it is."

Frank knew he was thinking about Iola Morton. It wasn't something Joe talked about very much, but Iola's death had left a scar that would never fully heal. When she was killed by a bomb meant for the Hardys, Joe had turned his grief into determination to find and punish those responsible for her murder. The trail had led to an international terrorist group known simply as the Assassins, and Frank and Joe had thwarted the Assassins' plot to murder a man running for president of the United States.

Frank's own girlfriend, Callie Shaw, frequently helped the Hardys on their investigations, and Frank often told Callie things that he would never tell anybody else. So he could hardly blame Gina for being careless or betraying their confidence.

"I think we both understand," Frank said. "Now let's just deal with the facts. How well do you know Solomon Mapes?"

Gina smiled. "Well enough to fall for him in a big way. I met Solomon a few weeks ago when I started working at Eddings. I don't know his whole life story, but I think I know him better than most people do."

"So you're pretty serious about this guy?" Frank asked.

"Very serious," Gina responded. "We have big plans."

"What kind of plans?" Frank prodded.

"Solomon isn't going to be a plain old pilot for the rest of his life," Gina explained. "He won't even be at Eddings that much longer. He's going to start his own air freight company, and I'm going to help him." She stopped abruptly and put her hand over her mouth. "Oops," she said with an embarrassed smile. "I wasn't supposed to tell anybody. I guess I'm not very good at keeping secrets. I probably wouldn't make a very good detective after all."

"An air freight company," Joe said. "Won't it take a lot of money to start a business like that? I mean, you need planes, right? And planes aren't exactly cheap."

Gina shrugged. "I don't really understand the details. Solomon only has to put up part of the money. He'll get the rest from financial backers."

"Still," Frank said, "I bet he'll have to come up with a big chunk of change himself before he can convince anybody else to back him."

"Solomon knows what he's doing," Gina responded a little defensively. "He's ambitious, but I think that's a good quality."

"As long as he's not *too* ambitious," Joe remarked.

After a few more questions, Frank concluded that Gina either didn't know or wasn't going to tell them anything about Solomon Mapes that might link him to the thefts. Joe was reluctant to leave, and Frank had to throw several large hints at him before he managed to steer his brother out the door.

"I hope we weren't too hard on her," Joe

said as they got in the car. "First we get her to confess to some petty crimes in her past, and then we grill her about her boyfriend. If we find out that Mapes is running this operation, I hope I'm not the one to break the news to Gina."

Frank sighed. "I hope I'm not the one who has to break the news to you if we find out Gina's involved. I know you like her. I like her, too—but we can't let that cloud our judgment."

"Why are you so suspicious of her?" Joe snapped. "I think she's being straight with us."

"You're entitled to your opinion," Frank shot back. "I'm not saying Gina is guilty of anything, but nothing she said just now makes her any less of a suspect than she was an hour ago."

Joe glared at his brother for a minute. He knew Frank was right, but he hated to admit it. "Okay," he said flatly, his gaze shifting to the road in front of the car. "Let's concentrate on our next move."

"We need to find out more about Mapes," Frank said. "Something about Gina's story doesn't make sense. When we first met Mapes, Eddings told us he wanted to start up an air freight division for Eddings Air. So why the decision to go solo?"

"That's a good question," Joe replied.

"But besides checking out Mapes, we have to find out more about Forrester," he added. "If he's taking bribes to forge employee records, he could be involved in heavier stuff, too."

Frank nodded. "He's in the perfect position to cover up any evidence that might point to the ringleaders of the luggage theft ring."

"Do you think we should tell Eddings?" Joe asked.

"Not yet," Frank answered. "All we have is Gina's word against Forrester. We need hard evidence before Eddings would listen to any charges against his security chief." He paused for a second. "But I definitely think it's time we had our meeting with Eddings. He said we had to talk soon. I can't think of anybody who could tell us more about Mapes or Forrester."

Frank reached Eddings on the phone around the time Joe's stomach started grumbling for dinner. Eddings suggested they meet in the park by his house again.

Eddings was pacing impatiently by the duck pond when Frank and Joe got to the park. "I heard there was some kind of accident when you were loading bags into a plane today," Eddings said.

Frank and Joe exchanged a glance. The last thing either one of them wanted to tell Eddings was that someone had engineered the "accident." He had already warned them that he would pull them off the case if it got too dangerous.

"Who told you?" Frank asked.

"Forrester told me," Eddings answered. "The foreman filed an accident report and sent a copy to Forrester. It's standard procedure." He turned to face Joe. "It *was* an accident, wasn't it?"

Joe chose his words carefully. "It looks that way."

"Hmm," Eddings responded. "I have a feeling there's something you're not telling me, but we'll drop that for now. Fill me in on what you've learned the past couple of days."

After the boys answered his questions and concerns, he asked what they wanted to see him about.

"We just need a little more background information on Eddings personnel," Frank said.

"Why come to me?" Eddings asked. "Talk to Forrester."

"Actually," Frank responded, "Hank Forrester is one of the people we wanted to know about."

Eddings raised his eyebrows. "Oh? What do you want to know?"

"Just routine background information," Frank said casually.

"I see," Eddings said slowly. He began pacing again. "Forrester is a good man. He was a career air force officer. He wanted to be a fighter pilot, but he didn't make the grade. So he did a little of everything from aircraft maintenance to design, and he eventually went into air force security. He came to Eddings Air when he retired from the service."

"What about Solomon Mapes?" Joe asked. "What can you tell us about him?"

Eddings snorted. "Solomon is a completely different story. He'd never last a day in the air force. He couldn't hack the discipline.

"What he lacks in maturity he makes up in talent and drive," Eddings continued. "And he's one of the best pilots I've ever seen. But flying isn't enough for Solomon. He wants more. But I'm not ready to give it to him— not yet. I've just decided he's too young and inexperienced to head up our new freight division." Eddings stopped talking abruptly and glanced sheepishly at the Hardys. It seemed to Frank as though Eddings felt he had revealed too much.

"Can you give us anything else on Mapes?" Joe asked.

"Nothing that would help you," Eddings replied.

"We won't take up any more of your time," Frank said. "Thanks for the information."

Eddings waved vaguely as the Hardys departed, his face turned toward the pond.

"What do you think?" Joe asked his brother as they ambled back to the car.

"I think we have a motive for Mapes now," Frank said. "If the freight division for Eddings Air was Mapes's idea and Eddings isn't going to let him head it up, then Mapes is probably pretty angry. I think part of his plan is to compete with Eddings. I'm also thinking about how Mapes knew we took the luggage."

"He'd have to steal a whole lot of luggage to finance an air freight company," Joe remarked.

"True," Frank conceded. "But Gina said he only had to put up part of the money. Bank loans and other investors might be supplying the rest."

They stopped at a restaurant and grabbed a late dinner before heading back to Danny's. By then it was late.

An hour later the phone ran at Danny's, waking them both.

"Where have you been?" a man's voice snapped in Joe's ear before he had a chance to say hello.

"You're not my mother," Joe retorted. "So why should I tell you?"

"We're tired of fooling around with you punks," the man said tersely. "We want that luggage."

"I told you before it would take some time," Joe replied.

"Your time is up," the man said.

"I'm shaking in my boots," Joe responded glibly. "What are you going to do? Kill us? Then you'll never get your luggage."

There was a dry, ominous chuckle on the other end of the line. "We're not going to touch you—not yet, anyway. We've got who we want. Gina Abend. If you don't do exactly what I tell you to do, the next time you see her, she'll be laid out in the morgue."

Chapter

13

THE WORDS HIT JOE like a punch in the stomach. Frank saw the color drain from his brother's face and knew something was very wrong.

Joe covered the receiver with his hand. "They've got Gina," he said.

"Are you sure?" Frank whispered. "Get proof. Tell them you want to talk to her."

Joe spoke into the phone. "Put Gina on the line. I want to make sure she's all right."

There was no response on the other end. Then Joe heard a small, frightened voice that sounded far away. "Joe? Frank? Please do whatever they say."

The gruff man's voice returned. "Satisfied?"

"Okay," Joe said, struggling to keep his voice steady. "You're in charge."

"Remember that," the man replied, "and the girl will keep breathing. Are the bags still at the airport?"

"Yes," Joe answered.

"Good. Be on the train that runs between the concourses at five A.M. Enter at Concourse D, and we'll meet you on the train. You can show us where you hid the stuff."

"Bring Gina," Joe responded. "Otherwise, no deal."

"You forget so quickly," the cold, flat voice said. "*I'm* calling the shots. Just be on the train. Don't tell anybody else. Don't bring anybody with you. Try anything funny and the girl dies."

There was a hollow click, and Joe knew the line was dead.

"Five in the morning on the automated train at the airport," Joe told Frank.

"That gives us a little more time to find out who we're dealing with," Frank said.

"Where do we go from here?" Joe responded.

Frank picked up the phone book and flipped through it. "Here we go. Mapes, Solomon." He wrote down the address.

Joe frowned. "Do you think Mapes would kidnap and threaten to kill his own girl-friend?"

"It doesn't seem very likely," Frank admitted. "But who else knew about the luggage that we took?"

Joe shrugged. "Nobody, as far as we know."

"There's also another possibility," Frank said.

Joe looked at his brother. He knew how Frank's mind worked. "I know," Joe said with a sigh. "If Gina's involved in the theft ring with Mapes, they could have faked the kidnapping."

Frank nodded.

"I still think Gina's innocent," Joe said. "We don't have much choice anyway—if they're not bluffing and we don't deliver the bags . . ." His voice trailed off.

"Don't worry," Frank replied. "We won't let anything happen to her. We just have to keep one step ahead of them, that's all. And the first step is to drop by Mapes's house to see if he has any plans for the rest of the night."

The Hardys found Mapes's house in one of the newer housing developments that had grown up on the outskirts of the city, not far from the airport. Joe drove slowly by the red brick ranch house, pulled into a driveway near the end of the block, turned around, parked, and killed the headlights.

"The lights are on," Frank observed.

Joe nodded. "And there are two cars in the driveway. It looks like Mapes is doing a little late-night entertaining." He glanced over at his brother. "Want to join the party?"

Frank and Joe slipped quietly out of the car and walked down the sidewalk like a couple of locals out for a late-night stroll. As they neared the redbrick house, the front door swung open, spilling a rectangle of light into the darkness. Frank darted behind a huge flowering bush, and Joe scrambled after him.

Peering around the side of the bush, Joe saw four figures emerge from the house. Even though they were cloaked in shadow, he instantly recognized one of them. "Gina!" he gasped. "And that's Mapes next to her. But I don't know the other two. Do you?"

Frank squinted to get a better look at the two tall, wide men behind Gina and Mapes. They were both wearing baggy business suits, and one of the men had several days worth of beard. Frank thought he looked like a well-dressed bum. There was something naggingly familiar about him, too.

Frank studied the men as they walked toward one of the cars parked in the driveway, a black, four-door sedan. One of the strangers got in the front passenger seat, next to Mapes. The other got in the back with Gina.

"The guy who needs a new razor," he whispered to Joe. "I think he was driving the Lincoln that tried to run us off the road."

"It looks like they're working for Mapes," Joe responded.

Crouching low and trying to keep bushes and trees between them and the car in Mapes's driveway, Frank and Joe ran back to their rented car. The black sedan pulled out of the driveway and swung in the Hardys' direction, the glare of the headlights piercing the windshield of the parked car. Joe ducked down, almost bonking heads with his brother, who dived for cover at the same time.

After the sedan had passed, Joe started the engine and cranked the wheel in a tight U-turn. He hung back and waited for the black car to go around a corner before he flicked on his headlights and followed.

Joe kept a healthy distance between the two cars. He had tailed enough suspects to know how to do it without being spotted.

"I wish we could get a closer look at them," Frank said. "When they came out of the house, nobody was holding Gina, and it didn't look like she was forced into the car."

"That doesn't mean anything," Joe said. "The two big guys might have had guns hidden in their suit jackets. We know one of them had a pistol."

"That's why I want to get a closer look. If

we can see how they're acting in the car, we'll get a better handle on the real situation."

Joe shook his head. "This late at night there's hardly any traffic—so we can't exactly blend in. If we get any closer, they'll spot us for sure."

The black sedan led them to the airport, where Mapes used a key card to enter an underground parking garage. The car disappeared inside, and the gate swung down, blocking the Hardys from following in their car.

"We could smash down the gate," Joe suggested.

"We could also set off some signal flares and yell, 'Hey, you guys! We're over here!' It's a concrete garage, Joe, and at this hour it's bound to be mostly empty. Any sound will echo from one end to the other."

Frank nodded out the window. "Park in that public lot over there. We'll go into the underground garage on foot."

Aware that they were losing precious time, Joe wheeled into the lot and parked haphazardly, not paying a whole lot of attention to fitting the car between the white lines. They both jumped out and sprinted back to the underground garage, slowing to a quiet jog as they moved through the garage.

They found the black sedan near the back of the first level. A quick glance told Frank the car was empty. There wasn't a soul in sight, and not even a single footfall disturbed the heavy silence.

Joe searched frantically with his eyes, not knowing what to do next. He couldn't help feeling that they'd let Gina down. "We've lost them!" he groaned.

"Time to regroup and plan our next move," Frank said. He glanced at his watch. "We have only a few more hours until the five A.M. deadline. Since we're already at the airport, we might as well stay here."

They headed into the main terminal and wandered down one of the wide corridors. The huge, nearly deserted terminal didn't do much to lift Joe's spirits. Here and there waiting passengers dozed in their seats, and Joe almost tripped over a guy about his age who was stretched out on the floor with a backpack as a pillow.

Frank pointed out a coffee shop that was open all night. Joe nodded, and they went in, sliding into a booth by a window that looked out into the terminal.

A waitress came over and put two menus on the table. Joe opened his menu and stared at it blankly. His stomach was grumbling—but not from hunger. It was the tension churning inside him.

Frank spoke to the waitress. "I don't think

we're ready to order yet. Could we have a few minutes?''

"Take your time," the woman said with a weary smile. "Just give a holler when you decide."

After watching the waitress walk back to the counter, Frank shifted his gaze to the window and out into the terminal. He wasn't focusing on anything in particular, and his mind was barely registering the few people who drifted past the coffee shop.

Then, out of the corner of his eye, Frank caught a glimpse of someone who made him snap his head around. A somewhat short and balding man walked across the terminal at a brisk pace, with a definite sense of purpose. He wore a drab gray suit, and his face was remarkably forgettable in every aspect.

It was a face Frank could never forget, though.

He bolted out of the booth and out of the coffee shop. More than a little startled, Joe jumped up and ran after him.

"What's going on?" Joe asked.

Frank stared down the empty corridor. In the few seconds that he had taken his eyes off the man, he had vanished. "This case was finally starting to make some sense," he murmured to himself. "Then *he* shows up."

Joe stared curiously at his brother. "Who?"

"Can you think of any reason why the Network would care about stolen suitcases?" Frank responded.

Joe frowned. "You're not making any sense."

"You're right," Frank said. "It doesn't make any sense. But I know what I saw."

Joe let out a frustrated sigh. "What did you see?"

"The most ordinary man in the world," Frank said. "The Gray Man."

Chapter

14

"THE GRAY MAN!" Joe exclaimed, peering up and down the corridor. "Where?"

"He was here just a minute ago," Frank insisted.

Frank ran over to a door marked No Admittance and tried the handle. It was locked. He dashed into the nearby rest room. It was empty. He walked out and stood in the middle of the long, wide corridor, scrutinizing the few people who moved about the airport at that hour. None of them looked as ordinary as the Gray Man.

"Well, he's not here now," Joe said. "Are you sure it was him?"

Frank thought about the unassuming man

who was a top operative for a secret government intelligence agency known simply as the Network. They first met him while tracking down the terrorists responsible for Iola Morton's death. Since then, the Hardys had helped the Gray Man out on several cases.

"I'm positive," Frank said firmly. "What I'm *not* sure about is the Network's connection to this case."

"It could just be a coincidence," Joe suggested.

"I don't trust coincidences," Frank said. "And when the Gray Man is involved, I get very nervous."

"We already have enough to worry about," Joe replied. "Mr. Gray can take care of himself. Gina is our top priority right now."

Frank and Joe covered as much of the airport as they could in the few hours remaining before their early-morning deadline. They prowled the corridors and tunnels for any clue that might lead them to Gina, Mapes, or the two men. The chances of finding them in the vast complex were remote at best, but Joe had to do something. Constantly moving was a way to vent some of his pent-up, restless energy.

At a few minutes before five, Frank and Joe headed for the underground train at Concourse D. Joe recalled that they had met Gina on the train their first day at the airport.

Frank knew they wouldn't have to wait long for a train. The computer-controlled electric trains shuttled back and forth between ticketing and the departure gates, less than five minutes were needed to cover the distance to the farthest concourse, a little over a mile from the ticketing terminal.

"This is where we split up," Frank said as he heard the train approaching.

"Split up?" Joe echoed. "What do you mean?"

"I'm going alone," Frank said. "We need some kind of plan, and this is it. Go back to the coffee shop. If I'm not there in half an hour, call the police, Michael Eddings, the national guard, or anybody else who will answer the phone this early in the morning."

"No way," Joe said, shaking his head. "I'm not letting you take on those guys alone."

"It's the only way," Frank said forcefully. "Think about it. If they're willing to kill Gina, do you think they'll think twice about silencing all three of us?

"If they don't know where you are," Frank continued, "what you know, or what you might do, they'll have plenty of reasons to think twice."

The train rolled to a stop, and the doors slid open. A few passengers got off as Frank stepped aboard. He turned around to wave to his brother, but Joe was already gone.

Frank was alone in the car until the train stopped at the next concourse, where Mapes, Gina, and their two escorts got on. One of them held Gina's arm in a rough grip. Gina's eyes were pleading with Frank to help her. That seemed to cinch it for Frank—she *was* being held against her will.

Mapes's eyes kept darting around nervously. In contrast, the two strangers studied Frank with cool detachment. The man with the stubble calmly approached Frank and frisked him.

The other stranger whispered something to Mapes. "Where's your brother?" Mapes asked.

"He couldn't make it," Frank said. "He had a previous engagement."

"This is no time for jokes," Mapes snapped. "Where is he?"

"He's in a nice, safe, public place." Frank glanced at his watch. "If Gina and I don't join him there in the next twenty-five minutes, you'll never get out of this airport."

"What kind of stunt is this?" Mapes demanded, panic in his voice.

"Think of it as an insurance policy," Frank said.

The train stopped and a few more passengers got on. The man who didn't like to shave moved closer to Frank and gave him a glimpse of a gun tucked in a shoulder holster under his suit jacket. Frank nodded. He got the message. If he pushed these guys too far, the consequences could be deadly.

The train slowed as it neared the ticketing terminal. "This is our stop," Frank announced, and led the way.

Joe darted out of the rear car of the train just as the doors started to close. In typical fashion, he had rejected Frank's plan and improvised, jumping onto the last car at the last possible moment. He watched at every stop until Frank got off with Mapes, Gina, and the two thugs.

Since everybody got off at the main terminal, it was easy for Joe to hide even in a small group. Most of the passengers headed for the baggage claim area, but Frank and company turned off into a side corridor. Two men, both wearing nylon jackets, apparently didn't know which way to go and trailed after Frank's group instead of following the other departing passengers. Sooner or later they had to realize they were going the wrong way. Until then, Joe took advantage of their confusion and used them as cover.

When Frank, Gina, Mapes, and the two suits went through a double swinging door with a sign that declared Eddings Air—Employees Only, Joe thought the two guys behind them would leave for the baggage claim. To his surprise, they went through the door, too. Joe decided to get a closer look at the men and picked up his pace. As he pushed open the Employees Only door, he realized his mistake—too late. Joe found himself staring down the dark barrel of an automatic pistol.

Frank reached the storage room and nodded toward the door. "This is it."

Mapes opened the door, stepped inside, and flipped the light switch. "It's a trick," he said. "This room is full of cleaning stuff."

"We hid the luggage in the back," Frank responded.

The man holding Gina dragged her into the room. The other silent stranger took out his pistol and motioned Frank inside, too. The man with the gun then closed the door.

"All right," Mapes said. "Where are the bags?"

Frank gestured to the two drums of cleaning fluid. "Behind those."

The man with the gun nodded to his companion, who let go of Gina and started pawing through the pile of suitcases, tossing them aside one by one without looking inside. He stopped when he reached the long, slender fishing-rod case.

Frank stared at the leather bag. What was

going on here? He seriously doubted that he had stumbled on a vicious gang of fishing-rod thieves.

The man took the top off the case, peered inside, nodded briefly to his partner, and put the top back on. Gripping the rod tightly in one hand, he brushed past Mapes and reached for the door handle.

"Hey, wait a minute!" Mapes exclaimed, grabbing the man's shoulder and spinning him around. "Where are you going? We had a deal. I had a nice operation going here until you came along. You got what you wanted. Now I want what's coming to me!"

The man reached into his jacket. Frank saw a brief flash of steel. Without a word, without so much as a blink, and without the slightest hesitation, the man raised a hand and struck at Mapes. Mapes staggered backward, his hands clutching his chest, blood seeping between his fingers. He stared down at the knife wound in wild-eyed horror, stumbled to his knees, and fell over onto his side.

The man with the knife turned to Frank and Gina. The cold gleam in his eyes told Frank that the two mute strangers had no intention of leaving any witnesses.

Chapter

15

JOE HAD NO IDEA that the situation down the hall in the storage room had just turned ugly. All he knew was that his brother might need him, and a couple of clean-cut guys wearing nylon jackets and shiny shoes were standing in his way. The fact that one of them was leveling a gun at him complicated the matter, and Joe hated complications.

"Don't move," the man with the gun ordered. "Put your hands in the air."

"Make up your mind," Joe responded sharply.

The man frowned. "About what?"

"I have to move to put my hands in the air, don't I?" Joe said.

The gun wavered as the man glanced at his partner. Joe didn't wait for a written invitation. He lunged forward and slammed into the man, bringing one of his arms down hard on the hand holding the gun.

"Hey!" the startled man yelled as the weapon flew from his grip and clattered on the concrete floor.

Joe shoved him into the wall and sprinted down the corridor.

"Halt!" a voice behind him barked.

Joe didn't even pause. The unexpected appearance of these two new players made him even more worried about Frank and Gina. He had to make sure they were all right.

Frank heard shouting and footsteps thumping down the corridor. Somebody was running toward the storage room. The man coming at Frank with the knife heard the commotion, too. He stopped to glance at his companion. The man with the gun opened the door a crack and peered out.

Frank made his move. His right foot lashed out in a karate kick aimed at the guy with the knife. The man reacted almost instantly, twisting out of the way and deflecting the blow with the fishing-rod case he was holding in his other hand. Frank hit the case with enough force to knock it loose. It skittered across the floor, and the man dived after it.

Frank spun around to confront the guy with the gun. The unshaven man was still standing by the door, but now he was facing Frank, the pistol held in a two-handed firing grip, aimed at Frank's head.

The door flew open just then and crashed into the man's back. The man stumbled forward, the gun discharged, and Frank flinched. A bullet whizzed past his ear and slammed into one of the barrels of cleaning fluid with a solid *ka-thunk*. Sudsy white liquid spurted out of the ragged hole in the metal canister.

Joe stumbled into the room. "Frank!" he called out. "Are you okay?"

"Look out!" Frank shouted. "He's got a gun!"

"He's not the only one!" Joe yelled back.

The man who had stabbed Mapes scrambled up off the floor, his knife forgotten, the fishing-rod case grasped in both hands. He dashed toward the door and collided with Joe. They both went down in a heap. The man with the gun grabbed the back of his companion's suit jacket, yanked him off Joe, shoved him out the door and rushed out after him.

"Freeze!" someone shouted down the corridor.

Several gunshots rang out in reply. Joe caught a glimpse of the two guys in nylon jackets as they darted past the open door, hot on the trail of the mystery men in suits.

Gina sank to the floor and cradled Solomon Mapes's head in her lap. "You're going to be all right," she said softly.

Mapes stared up at her. "A setup—" he gasped. "Why did—" He groaned and clutched at the gash in his chest.

"Hush," Gina said in a soothing tone. "Save your strength."

"I'll get a doctor," Joe said.

"A medical team is already on the way," someone behind Joe replied.

Joe turned to see the Gray Man standing in the doorway. The nondescript man in the plain gray suit walked into the storage room and knelt down next to Mapes.

"Mapes," the Gray Man said, "can you hear me?"

Mapes nodded weakly.

"It looks like your pals double-crossed you," the Gray Man said. "Here's your chance to return the favor. Tell me about them."

"Can't you see he's hurt?" Gina snapped. "Leave him alone!"

Mapes focused past the Gray Man, on Frank. His lips started to move, but no words came out. His teeth clenched in a fleeting grimace. Then his jaw went slack and his eyes closed forever.

Gina clasped him close to her and rocked

gently back and forth. Joe's heart went out to her as he watched her tears flow.

The two clean-cut guys came into the room. The Gray Man had a brief, whispered conversation with them, then motioned for Frank and Joe to join him outside in the corridor.

"You two certainly have a talent for getting in the way," the Gray Man remarked when they were alone.

"Nice to see you again, too," Joe responded.

Frank tried to mediate. "We're here because—"

"I know why you're here," the Gray Man cut him off brusquely. "Unfortunately, by the time I found out, it was too late to pull you off the case. Now it looks like you've fouled up an important Network operation."

Frank studied the Gray Man's bland face. "Why would the Network be interested in a luggage theft racket?"

The Gray Man paused. Frank knew he hated to reveal even the smallest bit of information.

"Come on," Joe said. "We have a right to know."

"Don't push your luck," the Gray Man said flatly. "I could have you arrested on half a dozen charges, starting with assaulting a federal officer."

Joe snorted with disgust. "Give me a break.

That guy didn't tell me he was a Network agent when he waved his gun in my face. You'll never make the charge stick.''

"No," the Gray Man admitted, "but I could make your life very uncomfortable for a while."

"Why are you coming down so hard on us?" Joe grumbled.

"We stumbled onto something really big, didn't we?" Frank ventured.

The Gray Man didn't reply.

"Is it the Assassins?" Frank prodded.

The Gray Man sighed. "If I don't tell you, you'll keep poking around until you manage to get yourselves into really deep trouble." He moved farther away from the storage room, gesturing to the Hardys to follow. "The Assassins were using the luggage theft ring to smuggle equipment around the country."

"What kind of equipment?" Frank asked.

"That's all I can tell you," the Gray Man said.

"That's all you can tell us?" Joe shot back bitterly. "There's a dead man lying on the floor back there. We almost got ourselves killed, and that's all you can tell us?"

Joe's words prompted Frank to ask another question. "Was Mapes a member of the Assassins?"

The Gray Man shook his head. "No—at least we don't think so. The Assassins don't give up their secrets easily. That's one of the reasons this operation was so important."

Frank raised his eyebrows. "*One* of the reasons?"

A glimmer of a smile touched the Gray Man's lips. "You don't give up, do you? I know you boys mean well, but leave this one to the pros, okay?"

The three of them walked back to the storage room, where Gina was still holding Mapes's head in her lap. Tears streaked her cheeks.

Painful memories of Iola flooded over Joe. "So what happens now?" he asked, trying to focus on the present, not the past.

"Take the girl home," the Gray Man said. "My men will take care of Mapes."

After Frank and Joe took Gina home and got one of her friends from the apartment complex to keep her company, they went to see Michael Eddings at his office. Even though no other employees were in yet, Eddings was already busily working at his desk.

"I know why you're here," Eddings said in a somber tone before Frank or Joe said anything. "The Gray Man briefed me a few minutes ago. If I had known it would end this way . . ." His voice trailed off.

"Did you know about the Network operation?" Frank asked.

Eddings nodded. "The Gray Man contacted

me yesterday. It still sounds unreal to me. How did Solomon Mapes get involved with a bunch of international terrorists?''

"Good question," Frank responded. "Did anybody else know the Gray Man was here on the trail of the Assassins?"

"Only Hank Forrester," Eddings replied. "He arranged security passes so the Network agents could get into restricted areas." He stood up and shook hands with Frank and Joe. "With Mapes dead, that should be the end of the luggage theft ring. You boys did quite a job. I'm almost sorry to see you go."

"Where are we going?" Joe asked.

"Home, I would imagine," Eddings said. "Now that the case is solved, there's no reason for you to stay in Atlanta any longer."

"If it's all the same to you," Frank said, "we'd like to hang around for a few days. We really haven't had a chance to see the city."

Eddings smiled. "Of course. Take your time. Just give me a call when you're ready to leave, and I'll make sure you get first-class seats on the first available flight."

Eddings returned to the pile of papers on his desk as the Hardys left the office. Joe almost bumped into Gina as he stepped out into the corridor.

"What are you doing here?" he asked gently. "Shouldn't you be resting or something?"

Gina smiled weakly. "I tried to sleep, but I

couldn't. After everything that's happened, I figured you'd be leaving.'' She stared up into Joe's eyes. ''I didn't get a chance to say good-bye to Solomon, and I didn't want you guys to disappear without some kind of farewell.''

''We're not going anywhere for a while,'' Frank said. ''This case isn't over yet.''

''It isn't?'' Joe responded with surprise.

''Think about it,'' Frank said. ''If Mapes was running the luggage theft ring, who sabotaged Eddings's private jet? Would Mapes deliberately damage the landing gear when he knew he was going to be flying the plane himself?''

''I hadn't thought about that,'' Joe replied. ''And Mapes told us about the sabotage. If he was responsible, he'd try to cover it up.'' He paused and frowned. ''So who sabotaged the plane—and why? Was it the Assassins? But why would they want Eddings dead?''

Frank looked at his brother. ''Eddings told us Forrester was supposed to fly to Bayport for the meeting with Dad, but he backed out at the last minute.''

Joe nodded. ''That's right—and his air force background would give him the expertise to make the sabotage look like an accident.''

''None of that tells us *why* he would do it,'' Gina pointed out.

''Maybe Solomon found out that Forrester was taking payoffs to forge employee records,''

Frank ventured, "and Mapes was blackmailing Forrester."

"Are you saying Forrester had Solomon killed?" Gina responded.

Frank shook his head. "The guys who killed Mapes aren't common hired hitmen. They must be Assassins.

"The whole picture is still a little fuzzy," he continued. "But if we can find some evidence linking Forrester to the sabotage, we can fill in the details later."

"Let's go down to the hangar where Eddings's jet is stored and ask a few questions," Joe suggested.

It took a while to find the hangar, and they had a few problems getting inside. Even though the Hardys still had their Eddings ID cards, they had difficulty explaining why a couple of baggage handlers needed to see Michael Eddings's private jet.

"We can't let just anybody come stomping in here to gawk at Mr. Eddings's plane," the mechanic who barred the door explained.

"So access to the plane is restricted?" Frank responded.

"You bet," the mechanic said. "And that's not all. A few weeks ago the security guys started checking the plane whenever Mr. Eddings was going to fly somewhere. I guess they were worried about a crackpot sneaking a bomb on board or something."

Frank and Joe exchanged a glance. "Did somebody from security check the plane before Mr. Eddings flew up to Bayport a few days ago?"

The mechanic thought for a moment and then nodded. "Yeah. The head of security, Hank Forrester, came down and personally inspected the plane."

Chapter

16

FRANK TURNED TO his brother. "I think it's time we had a little talk with the chief of security."

"What are we going to talk about?" Joe asked as they walked away from the hangar. "We don't have any proof that Forrester sabotaged Eddings's plane. We aren't even sure we have a motive."

"This is a switch," Frank remarked. "Usually you want to jump into action while I'm still poring over the details."

"I just think we need some kind of plan before we go barging in on Forrester," Joe said.

Frank smiled. "Don't worry."

Joe shot a sidelong glance at his brother. He knew what was coming next.

Frank's smile widened. "I have a plan."

"I *hate* it when you say that," Joe grumbled. "What's your brilliant idea this time? Dress me up like a girl and have me bat my eyelashes at him until he tells me his deepest secrets? Whatever it is, I'm not going to do it."

"If anybody has to do any eyelash batting," Gina spoke up, "I'll do it. If Forrester had anything to do with Solomon's death, I want to make sure he doesn't get away with it."

Frank saw the determination in her eyes. He didn't feel comfortable about Gina's joining them on the case, but he knew he couldn't convince her to stay on the sidelines. He also had a strong hunch that Joe would side with her if the issue came to a vote. So Frank shoved his concerns off to the side and concentrated on his plan.

The idea was still growing when they reached the Eddings Air offices. By the time Forrester finally agreed to see them, the scheme was complete.

"Okay, here's the plan," he whispered to Joe and Gina as they walked past the icy glare of the stiff receptionist. "I'll do the talking."

Joe waited for the rest of the plan. Frank didn't say anything else. Joe stared over at his brother. "That's it?"

141

Frank nodded. "Think you can handle your part?"

"Gee, I don't know," Joe muttered. "It sounds pretty complicated."

Forrester seemed to be annoyed when the three of them went into his office. "Don't hold your breath waiting for me to congratulate you," he said tersely. "You didn't make my job any easier. In fact, Mapes's death complicates the whole—" He stopped himself and looked at Gina. "I'm sorry," he said in a softer tone. "You were there, weren't you?"

Gina gave a slight nod. "He died in my arms."

"That's what we wanted to talk to you about," Frank cut in. "Since you're the head of security, we thought we should tell you what Mapes told us just before he died."

Forrester leaned back in his chair and frowned. "I heard he died almost instantly."

"He hung on for a few minutes," Frank replied. "He was in pretty bad shape. He kept babbling something about sabotage, and Eddings's private plane, and some kind of proof he had at his house."

Forrester let out a deep breath. "I see. Did he say anything else?"

Frank shook his head. "No, at least not anything coherent. Like I said, he was in pretty bad shape."

"Yes," Forrester said slowly. "Chances

are he was suffering from some kind of delirium. I doubt if his rantings meant anything. Still, you can't be too careful, can you? I'll look into it."

"Shouldn't we tell the police?" Joe asked, jumping into the act.

Forrester stood up. "Yes, yes, of course. I'll contact them. I'm sure you're all anxious to put this tragic incident behind you. Don't worry about police reports or anything like that. I'll take care of everything."

After Forrester ushered them out of his office, Frank headed for the parking lot where they had left their rented car the night before. Joe was right on his heels, and Gina stubbornly insisted on coming along. With Frank at the wheel, Joe beside him, and Gina in the backseat, they drove out of the lot and pulled up next to the underground garage where the Hardys had followed Mapes.

"This is a private garage for executives," Gina explained. "Solomon had a parking spot here because he was Eddings's personal pilot. Forrester parks his car here, too."

"Do you know what kind of car he drives?" Frank asked.

Despite the day's events, Gina managed a soft chuckle. "He has a dark brown, two-door sedan with a spotlight mounted on the driver's side door. It looks just like an unmarked police car."

A few minutes passed. There was no sign of Forrester's car.

"I still don't understand what's going on," Gina said. "What do you think Forrester will do? Nothing you said in his office was true."

"Forrester doesn't know that," Frank pointed out. "If he has nothing to hide, he'll turn the information over to the police, and that will be the end of it."

"But if he's guilty," Joe added, "he'll want to get rid of the supposed evidence as soon as possible."

"I get it," Gina said. "We're waiting to see if Forrester goes to Solomon's house to look for the 'proof' that isn't there." She lapsed into silence for a minute.

Joe glanced back at her. He could tell that something was bothering her. "What's on your mind?" he asked.

"I was thinking about Danny and Ted," she answered. "What's going to happen to them when this is all over?"

"With a little luck," Frank said, "nothing will happen to Danny. I don't think he had anything to do with the theft ring. The silver luggage tags and the stolen jewelry in his apartment had 'frame' written all over them."

"And Ted?" Gina asked.

"That's different," Joe told her. "But if he

turns himself in, he'll probably get a light sentence."

"He can't run forever," Frank said. "Sooner or later, the law will catch up with him."

Gina leaned forward and pointed out the window. "It looks like you were right about Forrester. That's his car coming out now."

They followed the car for a while, but it didn't take long to confirm what they already suspected. "He's headed toward Solomon's house," Gina said.

Forrester parked in Mapes's driveway and hurried to the front door. Frank pulled over to the curb a few houses away and watched Forrester ring the doorbell, wait a few seconds, and then try turning the doorknob without success. He glanced around quickly, pulled something out of his pocket, stuck it in the lock, and wiggled it around.

"If I didn't know Forrester was such an upstanding citizen," Joe remarked, "I'd say he was using a lock pick to break into Mapes's house."

"Security is his business," Frank said. "He knows all the tricks."

Forrester pushed the door open and slipped inside.

"What now?" Gina asked.

"Now we call the police," Frank answered. He wheeled the car around and drove to a gas station they had passed a few blocks back. At the pay phone, he punched in 911 and reported a break-in at Mapes's address. Then he jumped back in the car and drove back to the redbrick ranch house to wait for the police to arrive.

A few minutes later a squad car pulled up. Frank and Joe got out and went over to talk to the two officers, a gray-haired man and a young woman. Frank told them they had seen a suspicious character break into the house. The veteran police officer told them to stay clear of the area and then cautiously entered the house with his young partner.

Frank and Joe were just getting back in the car when they heard a muffled popping noise that sounded as if it was coming from inside the ranch house. The two brothers looked at each other. "That sounded like gunshots," Joe said.

Frank nodded. "Those officers may need some help. I don't think they called for any backup. You two stay here. I'll see if I can use a phone in one of these houses."

"Nobody lives in half of these places," Gina told him. "They're all brand-new homes. Solomon bragged about what a great investment it was, but I think the developers are having trouble getting people to buy the houses."

Frank looked around the neighborhood. The first time the Hardys had been to Solomon's house had been in the middle of the night. This time Frank had been too preoccupied with Forrester's movements to notice that most of the houses didn't have curtains on the windows, cars in the driveways, bikes on the front walk, or any of the typical signs that made a house look like a home.

"I'll just have to pound on doors until somebody answers," he said, and dashed off to the nearest house with any sign of life.

Joe slid into the driver's seat, and Gina moved into the front seat next to him. Joe had no idea what he would do if Forrester bolted out of the house, but he had no intention of sitting back and watching the man get away. He clenched the steering wheel and waited.

"Look!" Gina exclaimed, pointing at the house.

Joe's grip relaxed a little as he watched the gray-haired police officer back slowly out of the house, his gun drawn. Whatever had happened inside, the police now had the situation under control.

Joe's relief was short-lived. As the older police officer backed down the porch steps with his gun aimed at the front door, his young female partner emerged from the house with Forrester. But if the situation was under control, Forrester was the one controlling it—because he was holding a gun to the woman's head.

Chapter

17

JOE HELD HIS BREATH. It was a standoff between Forrester and the gray-haired police officer. The policeman had his gun leveled at Forrester—but Forrester was holding the woman officer in front of him and had a gun pressed against the side of her head. If Forrester fired, there was no chance that he would miss.

"You!" Forrester shouted to the older police officer. "Throw down your gun or your partner is dead."

Joe watched helplessly. Forrester's face was red and contorted. If he got any more rattled, he just might pull the trigger.

"Take it easy," the officer with the gun said in a steady voice.

Joe had to strain to hear the words from where he sat in the car a short distance down the block.

"Nobody's gotten hurt yet," the police officer continued. "Give up now, and it won't go that badly for you. Just put down the weapon and let Hemmings go."

"Not a chance," Forrester responded. "Throw your gun down in the grass right now or Officer Hemmings gets an early retirement."

"Frank should have found a phone by now," Joe whispered to Gina. "More police should be here any minute."

"I'm tired of dancing around," Forrester shouted, shoving the gun barrel harder against the woman's head.

"Now, just consider what you're doing," the gray-haired police officer said in a slow, even tone, his own pistol not wavering.

"Consider what *you're* doing," Forrester shot back. "You're signing your partner's death warrant. Believe me, I'll kill her before I'll let you take me in."

The police officer obviously believed him. He tossed his gun onto the lawn and raised both hands in the air.

Joe's sense of frustration and anger doubled as he watched Forrester force the two officers to sit on the sidewalk and bound them back-to-back with their own handcuffs. Joe glanced

149

up and down the street. "Where's Frank?" he muttered. "Where's the backup?"

His gun still pointed at the two on the ground, Forrester backed over to his car, whirled around to yank open the door, and jumped inside.

Joe couldn't believe it. Forrester was getting away! He reached across Gina and shoved her door open. "Get out!" he yelled, half pushing her out of the car.

As soon as she was clear, he started the engine and punched the gas pedal. The underpowered car didn't exactly rocket down the street, but it picked up speed as it homed in on the dark brown sedan backing out of the driveway of the redbrick house. Joe kept the pedal to the floor and rammed into the back side of Forrester's car with all the force he could coax out of the rented car.

The force of the collision knocked Forrester's car sideways. Joe jumped out of his car and dragged the stunned Forrester from the brown sedan before he had a chance to grab the gun on the seat beside him.

Joe heard the wail of sirens and looked up to see Frank and Gina running down the street, followed by a half-dozen squad cars with flashing blue lights.

After the two police officers were freed and the handcuffs were on Forrester, Frank stepped up to him. "Why did you do it?"

"Do what?" Forrester responded in a surly voice.

"Why did you sabotage Eddings's plane?"

Forrester glowered at him. "I don't know what you're talking about."

"Then what were you doing in Mapes's house?" Joe asked.

Forrester snorted. "I get it now. This was all a setup. Mapes didn't tell you anything. There isn't any proof of sabotage. You don't have a shred of evidence against me."

Frank shrugged, glancing at the two police officers who had tangled with Forrester. "Even if we can't prove you sabotaged the plane, there's plenty of evidence to convict you for assaulting a police officer."

"Make that assault with a deadly weapon and kidnapping," the gray-haired police officer spoke up. "That adds up to a long stretch behind bars."

Pizza was the main item on the menu that night at Danny Minifee's apartment, just like the first night the Hardys had spent there. But Joe couldn't help thinking how different things were now. Solomon Mapes was dead, Ted Nance was on the run, and Danny was facing charges for a crime he probably didn't commit.

Joe looked over at Gina. She was pale and subdued. She didn't say much except that she didn't feel like being alone. Joe knew she was thinking about Solomon.

Frank was about to say something to break the heavy silence in the room when the front door swung open. Frank and Joe both leapt up off the couch.

Danny Minifee stood in the doorway, a travel bag in one hand. Joe collapsed back on the couch. "You're lucky we didn't tackle you," Joe said with a sigh. "It's been that kind of day."

Danny shook hands with Frank and Joe. "I took your advice. I came back and talked to the police. I was ready to stand trial, but it looks like I won't have to."

"Why not?" Frank asked. "What made them change their minds?"

"They picked up Ted Nance a few hours ago," Danny explained. "He told them everything, starting with how he and Mapes framed me."

Danny looked at Gina. "Hey, in spite of everything, I'm still sorry about what happened to Solomon."

Gina struggled to smile. "I know he loved me. I'm sure those terrorists must have forced him to go along with them when they took me hostage. Solomon would never have hurt me."

Frank decided it would be cruel to disagree

with her at this point. "There are still a lot of unanswered questions," he said.

"It seems to me that everything's tied up in a neat bundle," Danny responded. "I don't know anything about any terrorists, but I can tell you Ted is naming names, nearly a dozen of them. Briggs is one of them."

Joe nodded. "We suspected that after he was so anxious to get us away from the scene of the 'accident' that nearly killed me."

Danny reached for a slice of pizza. "I haven't eaten all day. I'm starving."

"There's cold soda in the refrigerator," Frank told him.

When Danny was out of the room, Joe looked over at his brother. "What did you mean about unanswered questions?"

"For one thing," Frank replied, "why did Forrester sabotage Eddings's plane? Who was the target? Eddings? Mapes? You and me?

"And what was Mapes doing with a couple of Assassins?" Frank continued. He didn't mention the Gray Man's dubious explanation. He wasn't ready to reveal that much to Gina.

Joe knew what his brother was thinking. What was in that leather fishing-rod case that was so important to the terrorists?

"No matter what," Gina spoke up, "I'm going to find Solomon's killers. I owe him that much."

153

"We'll do it together," Joe said, putting his arms around Gina and Frank. "As far as we're concerned, this case is a long way from closed."

Frank nodded and glanced toward the kitchen. "For Danny it's over—but not for us."

Next in the Ring of Evil Trilogy:

Working undercover for an Atlanta airline, the Hardys have uncovered an international terrorist ring—the Assassins—bent on high-stakes smuggling and cold-blooded murder. But who is in control? What is their ultimate aim? Who will be the next to die? The dangerous truth lies in the rough and rugged wilderness of faraway Alaska.

The perilous passage north takes Frank and Joe into the heart of a titanic struggle. The Assassins are preparing to square off against the ultrasecret government agency, the Network, and it is a battle in which no one is safe—and no one can be trusted. Caught in a treacherous cross fire, the boys have only one ally, the beautiful Gina Abend, and even she may be leading them into a fatal trap . . . in *SURVIVAL RUN*, Case #77 in The Hardy Boys Casefiles™.

The future is in the stars . . .
the possibilities unlimited . . .
the dangers beyond belief . . .
in
the pulse-pounding new adventure

THE ALIEN FACTOR

A Hardy Boys and Tom Swift™
Ultra Thriller

Tom Swift has caught a falling star—a visitor from outer space who is as beautiful as she is strange. But his secret encounter has set off alarms at the highest levels of government. To check Tom out, a top-secret intelligence agency sends two of its top operatives: Frank and Joe Hardy.

But when the alien is kidnapped, Frank and Joe and Tom realize they have to work together. They're dealing with a conspiracy that stretches from the farthest reaches of space into the deepest recesses of their own government. The fate of the country and the planet could rest on uncovering the shocking truth about the girl from another world!

COMING IN JUNE 1993